THE
HOSTAGE

JAMES PATTERSON is one of the best-known and biggest-selling writers of all time. His books have sold in excess of 300 million copies worldwide and he has been the most borrowed author in UK libraries for the past nine years in a row. He is the author of some of the most popular series of the past two decades – the Alex Cross, Women's Murder Club, Detective Michael Bennett and Private novels – and he has written many other number one bestsellers including romance novels and stand-alone thrillers.

James is passionate about encouraging children to read. Inspired by his own son who was a reluctant reader, he also writes a range of books for young readers including the Middle School, I Funny, Treasure Hunters, House of Robots, Confessions and Maximum Ride series. James is the proud sponsor of the World Book Day Award and has donated millions in grants to independent bookshops. He lives in Florida with his wife and son.

BOOK**SHOTS**

STORIES AT THE SPEED OF LIFE

What you are holding in your hands right now is no ordinary book, it's a BookShot.

BookShots are page-turning stories by James Patterson and other writers that can be read in one sitting.

Each and every one is fast-paced, 100% story-driven; a shot of pure entertainment guaranteed to satisfy.

Available as new, compact paperbacks, ebooks and audio, everywhere books are sold.

BookShots – the ultimate form of storytelling. From the ultimate storyteller.

THE
HOSTAGE

JAMES
PATTERSON

WITH *ROBERT GOLD*

BOOK**SHOTS**

5 7 9 10 8 6 4

BookShots
20 Vauxhall Bridge Road
London SW1V 2SA

BookShots is part of the Penguin Random House
group of companies whose addresses can be found at
global.penguinrandomhouse.com

Penguin
Random House
UK

First published by BookShots in 2016

www.penguin.co.uk

A CIP catalogue record for this book is available
from the British Library.

ISBN 9781786530097

Typeset in Garamond Premier Pro font 12/16.5 pt in
India by Thomson Digital Pvt Ltd, Noida Delhi

Printed and bound in Great Britain by Clays Ltd, St Ives Plc

THE
HOSTAGE

PROLOGUE

Kensington, London, 2000

Everything was exactly as he'd said it would be.

Silently, he climbed the grand staircase, turning to his right when he reached its elegant summit.

He looked down the wide hallway.

The night light was on outside the boy's bedroom, as he'd been told it would be. He crept down the corridor and stood outside the dimly lit room. The door was decorated with the boy's own colourful drawings.

Inside, he could hear the child's gentle breathing. His anticipation grew and his heart beat faster. For a moment he froze, until his adrenaline pumped again and he stepped forward into the room.

There was no going back.

In one rapid movement, he scooped up the boy along with his soft, warm comforter. A second later he was back in the hallway, holding the boy and walking quickly towards the stairs.

Did he hear a noise? He quickened his pace.

Three steps from the foot of the stairs, the boy stirred.

He stopped. The boy stretched up an arm, turning his body, before almost immediately settling into a deep sleep once again.

A voice at the foot of the stairs told him to hurry. A flashlight pointed the way, down the hall and into the kitchen. Both men walked quickly. He followed the light through the kitchen, out of the back door of the house and into the pitch black of the night.

The late-winter cold hit him as he entered the garden and he instinctively wrapped the boy's comforter more tightly around his small, vulnerable body. Exactly as he'd been promised, none of the security lights were activated.

The flashlight pointed his way across the grass, through the shrubbery and onto the gravel track at the back of the house. As soon as he arrived, the waiting BMW opened its trunk and he stepped forward to lay the boy inside.

The boy was awake.

For the first time he panicked and clumsily bundled him into the dark space. He slammed the lid shut as the boy cried out for his mother.

Both men jumped into the rear seat of the car. The driver fired the engine, hit the accelerator hard and the car disappeared into the dark London night.

CHAPTER 1

Mayfair, London, 2016

Welcome, friends and honoured guests, to the brand-new Tribeca Luxury Hotel, here in the heart of the world-famous Mayfair district of London. Thirty years ago, in conjunction with my esteemed business partner, Oscar Miller, I opened the very first Tribeca Luxury Hotel in New York City. My aim today remains exactly as it was those thirty years ago – to deliver the ultimate in indulgence and service, set in the most opulent and tranquil surroundings.

When we opened our very first hotel, we placed our guests and the service we provided them at the very heart of everything we did. I am proud to say across our twenty-seven luxury hotels in operation around the world today, and of course in this, our twenty-eighth, that personal service remains. Every guest is treated as an individual and welcomed every time they visit as if they are returning to their very own home – the most luxurious home in the world.

In three days' time I will fulfil a lifelong ambition of opening a luxury hotel in Mayfair. For the very first time, we are bringing our unparalleled levels of exclusive accommodation, opulence and pure indulgence to the people of London and its international visitors. We take delight in offering our guests incomparable levels of comfort, consideration and security and our brand-new forty floors of palatial rooms are our finest demonstration of this yet.

I am honoured you are able to join us today at the exclusive preview of what I believe is the finest hotel in the world. Each one of you is my personal guest and I could not be more thrilled to welcome you to the new home of luxury in London, the Tribeca Hotel.

Jackson Harlington
Chairman, Tribeca Luxury Hotels

Stanley Samson stood in the marbled lobby and watched as each VIP guest was handed a branded magazine with a welcome letter from Jackson Harlington. This wasn't an event for ordinary travel writers. This wasn't even an event for the bosses of travel writers. This was an event for their bosses'

bosses. When it came to the grand opening of a Tribe__ __ux-ury Hotel, Stanley knew that everyone wanted to attend and no one wanted to be overlooked.

Browsing through the magazine, guests would find a feature on each of the group's luxury hotels located around the world, from New York to Paris, Singapore to Beijing. But it went without saying the greatest prominence was given to this brand-new London hotel. Gatefold photographs captured the beauty of the interior and the amazing accommodation available to the richest and most famous in the world.

Stanley was aware years of preparation had gone into this day. Every exclusive suite individually styled, every room its own unique furniture, selected and purchased by the world's most renowned interior designers. Flowers adorned the hotel, with fresh bouquets in every room. Private chefs had been appointed to every suite and individual butlers would serve every treasured guest. On the fortieth floor an oasis of calm had been created with an infinity pool offering commanding views across London and into the neighbouring royal palace gardens. No expense had been spared in preparation for the opening of the new hotel. Everyone in London was talking about it and nobody wanted to miss out.

Before it even opened its doors, the hotel was fully booked for the next two years. Fully booked – unless you were the President of the United States, a member of the royal family or a superstar of international fame. For them, Tribeca Luxury Hotels prided itself on always having a suite available.

As the assistant to the Global Head of Security for the luxury hotel group, Stanley was waiting by the express glass elevator to accompany Jackson Harlington, his family and his business partner, Oscar Miller, across the marbled lobby of the hotel to its majestic new front entrance. There, Harlington and Miller would throw open the doors and invite inside the world's press, as they had at the grand opening of every single Tribeca Luxury Hotel for the past thirty years.

Stanley never failed to be amazed by each Tribeca hotel he visited around the world. Every one of them offered a higher level of luxury than the last. For Stanley, the hotels were beyond his wildest dreams and he appreciated every night he got to stay in one of the rooms – even if it was in a room reserved for staff guests.

Being present at the opening of a hotel in his home town made him feel particularly proud. He knew the London hotel was certain to be an enormous success and was delighted to be playing his small part in it. He looked out across the lobby, through its vast glass frontage, at the gathering crowd standing on the front lawns. Hearing the string quartet play, he watched as guests reached for their glasses of vintage champagne and foie gras canapés. For a moment he felt a slight pang of jealousy but contented himself with the thought of the freshly baked chocolate muffins being delivered to the kitchen later in the morning.

But as he closely watched events on the front lawn, Stanley had failed to notice that the express elevator had journeyed from the twenty-fifth to the thirty-eighth floor.

With a ski mask pulled tightly down across his face, an uninvited guest was dragging his petrified hostage down the hall on the thirty-eighth floor towards the Presidential Suite. The hostage had been pistol-whipped by his captor and was drifting in and out of consciousness. As the captor clicked open the door to the lavish suite, his hostage began to stir and became aware of his surroundings.

The captor didn't care.

His hostage's arms were tied at his wrists and his legs bound at his ankles. He threw the man face down onto the suite's super king bed, made up with the world's finest Egyptian cotton sheets. The hostage struggled to try to turn himself over. But as he rolled himself breathlessly onto his side, he was greeted by the sight of his captor standing over him. Picking up a heavy-duty rope from beside the bed, he was tying a hangman's noose.

Panic flooded across his body. Trapped and tied, he was physically defenceless. He knew his only hope was to talk to his captor.

'Tell me what you want. If it's money I will get whatever you ask for. I'm a wealthy man. I can get you anything. Absolutely anything. Just tell me what it is you want.'

In silence the captor continued to tie the noose.

The hostage sat himself upright on the bed.

'I can get you cash here today. Or I can put you on a plane to anywhere. Anywhere in the world. You hear me? I've more money than you could ever dream of!'

The captor tightened the noose.

'I said, did you hear me?' screamed the hostage. 'I have more money than you could ever dream of.'

The captor walked to the bed and struck his hostage on the side of the head, throwing him back down.

The noose was tied.

'Tell me what you want! You must want something? Make demands. Make them now. I can pay you. I'll pay you anything!'

But the captor had slipped the noose over his head and was dragging him to his feet. The hostage cried for help but it was hopeless. With the exception of the invited guests gathering thirty-eight floors below, the hotel was empty.

Being pulled like a dog, with the noose choking his airway, the hostage followed his captor out onto the balcony of the Presidential Suite.

*

Thirty-eight floors below, standing on the carefully mani-
cured lawns, the gathering luminaries were being served the
finest caviar, flown in from Russia that morning. Savouring
every mouthful, their enjoyment was suddenly interrupted
by an ear-splitting crash. Looking skywards, they saw shards
of glass falling like ice towards the ground.

Standing on the edge of the balcony was a masked man
with a hostage tied in a noose. Slowly, the man raised his knife
and ripped through the shirt of his captive. In the gardens
below, guests began to scream.

Forcing his hostage to his knees, his arms above his head,
the captor tied his wrists tightly to the iron frame – all that
remained of the Presidential balcony.

He secured the noose.

Then, with one kick, he pushed his hostage off the edge
of the balcony, leaving the man hanging thirty-eight floors
above the ground.

CHAPTER 2

ON THE HOTEL LAWNS BELOW, cameras and smartphones turned upwards as the man swung from side to side. Stripped to his waist, his overfed figure exposed to the watching audience, he had no defence. Any attempt to escape now seemed futile, as he screamed in desperation at the crowd below.

Not wanting to keep his audience waiting, the masked man stepped forward and knelt closely beside his suspended hostage.

He was ready to continue the performance.

He raised his knife, its sharp blade glittering in the spring sun. The crowd gasped as, slowly, he pressed the knife against the man's face, letting it delicately cut his cheek as he edged it down towards his throat.

'Don't do this, don't do this,' gasped the hostage. 'It isn't too late. However much money you want I'll get it for you. Anything, absolutely anything. You can have it all. Do you hear me? Anything.'

The captor let the cold knife press deeper into his hostage's cheek before pushing his hidden mouth into his ear.

In a barely audible whisper, filled with hate, he spoke.

'That's a greedy gut, isn't it?'

He twisted the knife, dropping it down, cutting into the tight skin covering his hostage's obese stomach.

The hostage shrieked in pain as his captor rose up on his knees, reached skywards and showed the bloodied knife to the screaming crowd below.

It was time for the final act.

The captor pressed the knife against the rope that tied his hostage's wrists to the balcony frame. One cut of that rope and the man would be left hanging by the noose, thirty-eight floors above the ground.

The crowd gasped in fear and anticipation as the captor pressed harder and harder against the rope.

Then suddenly, sweeping the knife down to the hostage's stomach, he raced it back up through his torso, across his body, and spilt his entrails down towards the watching crowd below.

CHAPTER 3

TWO FLOORS BENEATH the main entrance to the new London Tribeca Luxury Hotel is situated the hotel's security control room. From this underground office, Global Head of Security for Tribeca Luxury Hotels, Jon Roscoe, and his team view every public space inside the hotel, allowing them to control and limit access to any area and to retrieve information from any of the hotel's high-definition video security systems.

For the grand opening of the new hotel, Roscoe had set up a standard launch protocol. While his assistant, Stanley Samson, would oversee the opening of the building from the inside, he would mix personally with the arriving guests while observing security checks at the front gate. Once all guests had arrived on site, he would head into the control room to observe the flow of dignitaries into the hotel. Access would then be granted to all public areas to allow visitors to explore the luxuries of the new hotel before official tours of some of the hotel's finest suites followed later in the day.

This was the fourth grand opening Jon Roscoe had over-seen since he'd joined Tribeca Luxury Hotels two years ago. Before joining the hotel group he had served as a member of London's Metropolitan Police for fifteen years, yet he didn't have a single day when he regretted resigning from the force.

Travelling the world to oversee security at the world's twenty-seven most luxurious hotels, while mixing with billionaire businessmen and superstar performers, was a whole lot more fun than chasing down criminals in the rainy backstreets of London on a cold November evening.

His new job came with its pressures, and Tribeca guests could be some of the most demanding in the world, but Jon was adept at handling any situation and never let the luxurious locations he worked in put him off his guard. He could go from dealing with the most powerful and high-profile government security forces in the world, when Tribeca hosted political leaders or members of royal families from across the globe, through to aggressive private security firms employed to shelter some of the new Eastern European mafia powerbrokers. All of them were challenging, but Roscoe knew he was an equal to them all and was happy to be part of the team delivering the ultimate in Tribeca Luxury Hotels' personal service.

The VIP arrival process had passed without incident. Roscoe grabbed a coffee as he headed from the gardens, through the lobby and down to the control room, taking his seat in front of the bank of video screens.

Something was wrong.

From the cameras positioned in the lobby and other key public areas, he could see all inside the hotel was calm. But outside he saw the gathered dignitaries had all turned to look up. Many appeared to be shading their eyes from the sun as they looked up at the roof of the building.

Fixed camera angles gave Roscoe a direct view of the front of the hotel as well as its grand entrance and glass windows, but he could see nothing out of the ordinary. He quickly turned to the cameras on the fortieth floor that gave a close-up view of the rooftop and its infinity pool. The whole area was deserted. Rapidly he flicked through the cameras pointing at all the public areas. None of them showed him what was caus-ing the crowd outside to behave in such a way.

Then he thought of the private guest areas.

He knew Tribeca policy was never to have any camera access to guest areas, as Jackson Harlington and Oscar Miller had made it clear that this space was sacrosanct. Guests at Tribeca Luxury Hotels were returning home to the ultimate in luxury. That meant they were free from the direct prying eyes of any security cameras.

Roscoe reached for the schedule giving him a minute-by-minute breakdown of the day's timetable. Had he forgotten about a rooftop event to kick off the day's proceedings? No – he knew the timetable back to front. He had written it. The day ended with fireworks on the fortieth floor but nothing was to take place outside the building before then.

He looked again at the crowd standing on the front lawns. Some were turning away, some now covered their eyes – but all seemed transfixed by events in the sky. Knowing something was wrong, Roscoe sprang to his feet, ran to the door and, grabbing his phone, headed up the two flights of stairs back into the lobby.

Sprinting across the hotel's marble lobby, Roscoe's ripped six-foot frame cut an imposing figure. He looked towards the elevator bank for his assistant Stanley, but Stanley was gone.

At the front entrance, the lobby manager of the new hotel, Anna Conquest, called across to him.

'Jon, what's happening?'

'I don't know yet,' said Roscoe as he keyed the security pad to open the front entrance.

'We heard screaming outside. Somebody must be hurt.'

'Have you seen Stanley?'

'He was waiting by the elevator for Jackson Harlington. Then the screaming started. I didn't see where he went.'

The front entrance opened and, seeing the chaos outside, Roscoe shouted to Anna to get the police to the hotel. 'Now!'

But it was too late.

As the watching crowd screamed again, then scattered, Roscoe looked up in horror to see a blood-covered body falling from the sky.

Roscoe ran across the lawn as the body crashed to earth, blood splattering the dispersing crowd. The garden and flowers that had been tended and trimmed to perfection were now sprayed with red. As he reached the obliterated body, he could see, even in its devastated state, that it was the remains of billionaire investor and Tribeca Luxury Hotels major shareholder Jackson Harlington.

CHAPTER 4

STANDING NEXT to the body of Jackson Harlington, Jon Roscoe turned to face the crowd. He held up his hands as he made a direct appeal.

'I need everybody to step back away from the body and away from the hotel, right now,' he commanded. 'I want everybody to move back into the gardens and I need everybody to stop filming.' Roscoe was unsure if his last request would be heeded but he pressed on. 'And I need to know specific information about what people saw.'

A woman screamed out, 'He cut open his body. Ripped open his stomach!'

'Did anyone see the attacker?' said Roscoe, trying to make himself heard above the panic coming from the crowd. 'Can you tell me, was there more than one person involved?'

'He was wearing a mask,' a voice called out.

'I've got a video here,' called another. 'It looked to me like he was on his own.'

'I could only see him. I don't think there was anyone else with him.'

Roscoe knew trying to get information in this way was hopeless. From the blood and entrails scattered across the garden, along with the state of Jackson Harlington's body, he knew a ferocious attack had taken place. He needed to get back inside the hotel to track the killer. He started to push his way through the assembled journalists and dignitaries, who were beginning to react with a mix of shock, morbid fascination and a desire to scoop the story. Even journalists and writers who spent their time reporting on the latest advances in luxury travel and on the world's most extravagant destinations realised they were suddenly part of a far bigger story. As Roscoe tried to make his way back into the hotel lobby, he found his route blocked by journalists peppering him with questions.

'Is that Jackson Harlington?' cried one.

'Who would want to kill Jackson Harlington, and in such a ferocious way?' asked another.

He felt one journalist grab his arm. 'Do you think the killer is still in the hotel? Maybe we can help you track him down. He'd have no chance against all of us.'

Roscoe wanted to lash out. This wasn't a game. He needed to get back inside the hotel. He needed to start the hunt for a killer.

'Is Mrs Harlington in the hotel? Is the Harlington family safe?'

The questions kept coming as he made his way through the crowd.

'Is Oscar Miller in danger? Do you think this is an attack on Tribeca Luxury Hotels?'

'I heard somebody's room service was delivered cold,' quipped one of the journalists, and a number in the crowd started to laugh.

'Yeah, I'd heard he hadn't got clean towels this morning,' called out another and the laughter continued.

Roscoe wanted to shout that a man lay dead a few feet away from them, a man they had all seen brutally murdered. How could they stand at the front of the hotel joking about Jackson Harlington's death? Human nature never failed to surprise Roscoe. Shock played its part, along with the madness of crowds, but it never ceased to amaze him how people could react to tragedy.

Ignoring all those around him, he pushed forward, through the crowd and into the lobby of the hotel, where confusion was taking hold. Anna Conquest was standing by the elevators, preventing anyone making their way further inside the building.

'Police are on their way,' she called as he hurried across the vast marble lobby.

'I'm locking down the elevators,' he shouted. 'Nobody goes beyond this point. I don't want people running round the hotel trying to be heroes. Anna, I've never seen anything quite so brutal.'

'Is it Jackson Harlington?'

'Afraid so.'

'He's dead?'

'He's dead all right. Cut open and his guts spilled out all over the front lawn.'

'My God. Who on earth would do that?'

'I've no idea, but I'm pretty sure whoever it was is still inside the hotel.'

Roscoe opened the elevator control pad, entered the emergency code, locking each of the hotel elevators in their current position. Stepping forward, he called out to the crowd gathering in the lobby.

'The hotel is in lockdown. No one should attempt to access any other part of the building. Do not go beyond the lobby. When the police arrive they will need to take witness statements from each of you. The killer is still at large and there is every reason to believe he's still inside the hotel. He is clearly an armed and incredibly dangerous individual. No one here should attempt to apprehend him.'

His heart pounding, he turned to Anna. 'The police will be here within minutes. If anything happens, call me.'

'Where are you going?'

'To catch a killer.'

'You've just told everybody how dangerous this man is,' said Anna, her voice trembling. 'Shouldn't you wait until the police get here?'

'I'll be okay.'

'Why? Because you're a little bit crazy?'

Roscoe smiled. 'Maybe a little bit.'

As he opened the door to the stairway beside the bank of elevators, Anna reached out, gently touching his arm. 'Be careful, Jon.'

Roscoe looked at her for a moment, and then started to run up the stairs.

Taking the steps two at a time, he made his way up to the fourth floor. At the next turn, he found Stanley Samson collapsed against the door leading to the hallway.

His shirt was soaked in blood.

CHAPTER 5

FROM THE MOMENT he'd met Stanley, Roscoe had recognised what a huge contribution he would bring to his team. His boundless enthusiasm and determination to do the right thing were combined with a sharp intelligence and a deductive mind. And when the two men had started working together, Roscoe had got to know and grown to respect a man who was always thinking ahead and ready to risk his own safety to get the right result.

Now, crouching at Stanley's side, Roscoe thought of how, since he'd been a small child, his friend had dreamt of becoming a police officer and working every day at New Scotland Yard. At the age of nineteen he'd applied to become a member of London's Metropolitan Police Service; at the age of twenty-one he'd applied for a second time; and at the age of twenty-three he'd applied for his third and final time. Each time Stanley had failed the force's physical – perhaps his love of chocolate-frosted doughnuts played no small part in his failure. Three months after his third failed application, however, Stanley had been recommended for a role as a civilian employee with the London police force, and after two interviews with Jon Roscoe he was in.

When Roscoe resigned from the Metropolitan Police and was soon after appointed to the position of Global Head of Security at Tribeca Luxury Hotels, he'd had no hesitation in offering the role of his assistant and de facto number two to Stanley. At first, Stanley had hesitated. He loved his job working with the police and perhaps still hoped one day he might become a commissioned officer. But two weeks of no longer working alongside Jon was all it took for Stanley to realise that while working in the Metropolitan Police might have been his dream, working with Jon had made it a reality, so he gave his notice and headed out of New Scotland Yard. Since joining Jon at Tribeca Luxury Hotels, Stanley had loved every single day, working on different challenges across the world. He simply couldn't imagine working with anyone else.

Minutes earlier, standing in the lobby of the new hotel and hearing the glass shatter on the floors above, Stanley had been the first to react. Recognising there was no help to be given outside the hotel, he had made his way up the stairs in the hope of finding the killer attempting an escape.

And that was when he'd heard the noise on the stairs above him: footsteps flying down the stairs, a body crashing from side to side as it made a rapid descent. With no time to react, Stanley decided to stand his ground. He quickly made his way up to the fifth-floor landing, giving himself the space to tackle the man head-on. While he might not be the quickest, he had the strength and weight to bring most men to the ground.

One-on-one, Stanley knew he could take the man down.

A man appeared at the top of the flight of stairs, wearing a black ski mask to conceal his face.

Jumping down three steps, he launched himself forward, knocking Stanley sideways. Stanley grabbed hold of the man's wiry frame, and the two grappled on the floor. Stanley felt the man wrap his hands around his throat and start to squeeze. Seizing hold of his adversary's arm, Stanley sensed the strength of the man but could tell he didn't possess the same basic power as he did. Turning his body, he flipped the man over and pushed himself free.

But the man was quick and jumped Stanley before he had a chance to recover. Suddenly the pair were rolling down the next flight of stairs, still locked in combat. They hit the fourth floor landing and Stanley was able to pin his opponent to the floor.

He had the man trapped.

And then a desperate, gut-wrenching pain ripped through his stomach and flooded across his body. He'd been stabbed. Stanley started to shake as pain poured through every sinew.

Powerless and unable to move, his strength ebbing away, he lay paralysed as the man ripped the knife out of his stomach and raced back up the building.

Seeing Stanley lying in the corner of the stairs, Roscoe knelt beside his friend. He lifted Stanley's head to speak to him, gently holding him in his arms. He could see immediately Stanley was badly hurt and was beginning to lose consciousness.

'Talk to me, buddy,' he said, desperately trying to keep Stanley awake.

'He went back up the stairs, Jon,' whispered Stanley, summoning all of his energy to speak. 'Go after him. Don't worry about me.'

'Not until we get you some help.'

'You can't let him get away.'

'I'll get him, but first off we've got to sort you out.'

'You're the best, Jon,' said Stanley, the pain surging through his body. Wave after wave swept across him. He closed his eyes, ready to embrace the darkness. Softly his head fell into Roscoe's arms and he drifted away.

'Stanley!' Roscoe cried, ripping off his jacket and bundling it up to support Stanley's head.

Stanley opened one eye. 'Can't a guy get any peace and quiet round here?'

'Thank God! I thought you were checking out on me. We're going to get you some help, buddy, I promise you.'

Carefully he opened Stanley's blood-soaked jacket, seeing the size and severity of the knife attack. Blood continued to ooze from the wound. He cursed himself for leaving Stanley alone to chase the killer, telling himself that he should never have gone outside. He was the one who knew how to stop a killer, not Stanley.

Roscoe tore off his shirt and pressed it onto Stanley's stomach in an attempt to staunch the bleeding. Stanley yelled out as the pain shot through him.

'It's okay, buddy. We've got to stop this bleeding.'

'It's not good, is it, Jon?' Stanley murmured.

'I said I was going to get you some help, and I will.'

Roscoe bent down and summoned all his inner strength. With a guttural cry he strained every muscle in his body and lifted Stanley into his arms.

Staggering under Stanley's not inconsiderable weight, he made his way down the four flights of stairs to the lobby. At the foot of the stairs, he kicked open the door and stumbled out. Carefully he lay Stanley down on the marble floor. As he did so he collapsed, exhausted.

Down on his knees beside his friend, Roscoe called out urgently across the lobby, 'Man down! I need help here right now.'

CHAPTER 6

COVERED IN SWEAT and smeared with Stanley's blood, Roscoe shouted again.

'I've got a stab victim. He needs immediate medical attention!'

Aware that his blood-covered T-shirt was sticking to his body, Roscoe staggered to his feet. Two paramedics raced across the lobby.

'He's been stabbed in the stomach,' he explained as the two women approached. 'I've tried to stop the bleeding, but he's still losing a fair bit of blood.'

As the paramedics knelt beside Stanley and started to tend to him, Roscoe took a step back. He felt dazed. He wanted to give them space to work on Stanley and to give himself space to think where he went next. Minutes earlier he was drinking a coffee and looking forward to the opening of the most prestigious hotel in London. Now he was standing in the lobby of that hotel, covered in the blood of one of his closest friends and colleagues, while the owner of the hotel lay dead on the front lawn. A killer was on the loose somewhere within the hotel's forty floors and he had no idea where. He knew the killer had been in the Presidential Suite because that was where Jackson Harlington had been killed. He knew the killer had access to private rooms. But where he would head next, Roscoe had no idea.

He looked out across the marbled lobby, a vast room filled with dignitaries and journalists. Some looked fearful, but all of them were waiting in anticipation to see what happened next. He had noticed a number of the journalists snapping pictures of him as he'd carried Stanley into the lobby, and he imagined them already appearing on Twitter feeds and news websites around the world. Hotel staff had started to congregate in the lobby, adding to the general levels of confusion. Roscoe realised if the killer could make it to ground level he might easily take the chance to slip away in the midst of all the chaos – that was, if escaping the building was what the killer wanted to do. But now he wasn't so sure. Why had he run back up into the hotel after attacking Stanley? Why not head for a way out?

Roscoe knew he had to try to get inside the killer's head; he needed to see his brutality close up. He wanted to see what had happened on the thirty-eighth floor.

'He's going to be okay, you know,' said Anna Conquest, making her way to Roscoe's side as he unlocked the elevator bank.

He turned to face the lobby manager, who even in a time of crisis seemed to him to radiate a calming beauty. 'Hey. I didn't see you there.'

'You were a million miles away. Stanley's in good hands now, Jon,' she continued, placing a reassuring hand on his back.

Roscoe breathed out and nodded.

'I know, but it should have been me, not Stanley, chasing down the killer.' He looked across at the paramedics still tending to Stanley. 'That should have been me.'

'You did everything you could. You went straight upstairs without a second thought.'

'I was wasting my time looking at video screens when I should have been out there,' said Roscoe, pointing towards the hotel gardens. 'But I'm not going to make that mistake again.'

'What are you doing?' asked Anna as the elevator doors opened.

'I'm going up to the Presidential Suite. I need to have an idea of what I'm dealing with.'

'Surely you should wait until the police get here?'

'Too late – they already are.' He gestured across the lobby and paused as he watched the Metropolitan Police enter the building. 'And look at the corrupt fool they sent us.'

CHAPTER 7

ROSCOE SEIZED ANNA by the hand, pulled her into the express elevator and hit the button for the thirty-eighth floor. As the doors closed in front of them, he could see Inspector Peter Savage looking directly across the lobby towards him. Roscoe's expression of indifference was intended as a direct challenge to the inspector.

'Jon, what about the police?' asked Anna as the elevator raced its way vertically through the building.

Roscoe grinned, readying himself for the chase.

'I need to see the Presidential Suite before that crook.'

'What crook?'

'Inspector Peter Savage of the Metropolitan Police. I worked with him for most of my fifteen years on the force. We never really got on. Well, I say we never really got on – we hated each other. He was one of the main reasons I quit. He's a bully and a cheat. He doesn't care how he gets his convictions. He'll intimidate witnesses to get them to say whatever he needs, and then if that doesn't work he simply plants his own evidence.'

'If he was so corrupt, wouldn't someone find him out?' said Anna.

The elevator reached the thirty-eighth floor and Roscoe led them down the hallway.

'I did. But the high-ups didn't want to hear it. Peter Savage delivers convictions so he's worth his weight in gold, whatever the collateral damage.'

Roscoe used his access pass to open the main door to the Presidential Suite. Stepping inside, he felt warm spring air blow through the room from the open balcony door. How different to the horrors that had taken place only a few minutes before, he thought. But as the curtains billowed into the room, his heart dropped as he saw their pure-white fabric had been daubed in blood.

Reluctantly, Anna followed Roscoe out onto the balcony, where she saw the remains of the rope the killer had used to hang his hostage from the balcony frame. Seeing the blood sprayed across the balcony floor, she knew she didn't want to see any more and stepped back into the suite. Thinking of the horror Jackson Harlington had suffered, she walked through into the suite's dining room, where she found beer bottles scattered across the table and a half-eaten supermarket sandwich sitting in the middle of a Royal Doulton china dinner plate.

'Jon,' she called as Roscoe made his way into the suite's main bedroom. 'In here.'

'Looks like he made himself at home,' said Roscoe, picking up the sandwich bag before dropping it back onto the table. 'Must have been here a while before he struck.'

'Shouldn't we wait for the police now?' asked Anna.

'Yes, he should,' said a voice at the suite door. Roscoe had been expecting it. 'I'd have thought retired inspector Jon Roscoe would have known better than to tamper with the evidence at a crime scene – unless, of course, he has something to hide.'

The last time Roscoe had seen Peter Savage had been on the day he'd resigned from the police force. The final case they'd worked on together had seen a casino security guard accused of assault and attempted murder. From the outset, Savage was certain the security guard was guilty. To him it was an obvious fit. A steroid-pumped security guard was an easy target to tailor for a conviction.

But Roscoe wasn't so certain.

Surveillance cameras both inside and outside the casino offered no conclusive evidence. For Savage, however, this meant a perpetrator who knew how to avoid being seen. It was simply a case of finding the evidence to convict his man and he ignored the fact that the two victims had been involved in a fight in a nearby pub earlier in the day.

No DNA evidence against the security guard existed until Savage was left alone to carry out a second sweep.

Suddenly the evidence materialised.

A conviction followed that Roscoe knew in his heart was dirty.

He raised an internal investigation with his superiors but it was swept away. The day the Internal Investigation Unit delivered its report was Roscoe's last day as a member of the Metropolitan Police. He resigned that day and never returned.

'Is this lovely lady checking in for the night?' said Savage, looking at Anna Conquest. 'You here to carry her bags, Roscoe? Sorry I'm not here for a longer stay myself or you could have checked me in as well – earned yourself a nice tip.'

'Don't start, Savage,' replied Roscoe, not putting any effort into hiding his dislike of the man. 'We've got one dead man and another one badly injured.'

'And a third man who has no jurisdiction, so butt out. I want you back down in the lobby right now.'

As they rode the elevator back down, Savage turned to Roscoe. 'You look bloody horrendous. What have you been doing?'

'Trying to catch a killer – while you were taking your time getting here.'

When the elevator doors opened on the lobby, Savage looked across at Stanley, still lying on the floor receiving treatment from the paramedics.

'What happened to the big man?'

Roscoe bristled at Savage's goading but Anna put her hand on his arm.

'He was stabbed in pursuit of the killer,' Roscoe said.

'Pretty *slow* pursuit's my guess,' Savage laughed. 'We'll need to speak to him before you take him away,' he continued, speaking directly to the two paramedics.

'Afraid we have to get him out of here as soon as he's stabilised,' replied the lead paramedic. 'He won't be speaking to anybody right now.'

'I can tell you what happened,' said Roscoe, standing beside the inspector. 'The killer was wearing a ski mask so we don't have a description. Stanley tackled him on the stairs, the killer pulled a knife and Stanley got stabbed. After that, the killer headed back up into the hotel.'

'So we're saying we've got this crazy guy running around somewhere upstairs but we have no real idea where?'

'Would seem like it,' Roscoe agreed.

Roscoe watched as Savage drew himself up, filling out his chest, as he readied himself to take control. He'd seen it a thousand times before.

'Then I want everyone in the building brought down to the lobby and they remain here until I say otherwise. Starting with you, Roscoe.'

CHAPTER 8

ROSCOE STEPPED ASIDE as, refusing to answer any questions, Savage and his team issued instructions to everyone in the lobby. No one was to leave the area. Confusion continued to reign and all those who only a few minutes before had appeared so eager to come inside the hotel now suddenly felt trapped.

Were they in danger or were they under suspicion? All of them were to be interviewed as witnesses and could not leave the building until statements had been taken. Roscoe knew that Savage would be determined not to be the one to let a killer slip through his fingers.

Voices began to be raised as guests expecting a four-course lunch accompanied by some of Europe's finest wines found themselves imprisoned inside the hotel, and the rising discontent became an audible aggression when a blanket ban on the use of all mobile phones was issued. How were they to report live on the developing story to the outside world, especially one they now found themselves at the centre of?

Roscoe watched tempers becoming increasingly frayed as Savage made threats of arrest in an attempt to gain control of the situation.

Roscoe was standing next to Anna Conquest as the phone on her lobby desk started to ring. She stepped across and picked up the handset. A hollow voice came on the line, and Roscoe heard it demand to speak to whoever was in charge. As she was trained to do, Anna politely asked who was calling but she and Roscoe already knew.

It was the killer.

She quickly beckoned to Roscoe, who moved across towards her but as he did so Savage jumped forward and attempted to snatch the phone from Anna's hand. Too quick for him, she moved the phone from one hand to the other and spoke to both men.

'He says he wants to speak to whoever is in charge.'

'Then that would be me, wouldn't it, Ms Conquest?' said Savage.

Roscoe nodded in the direction of Savage, indicating to Anna she should give him the phone.

'This is Inspector Savage of the Metropolitan Police. I'm the person in charge here.'

'I think you'll find, Inspector, *I'm* the person in charge now,' said the voice on the phone.

'Who is this?' asked Savage, anger rising in his voice.

'I'm the new hotel manager. I wanted to call you personally to remind you how much we pride ourselves in the special individual treatment each one of our very honoured guests receives here at Tribeca Luxury Hotels. Please rest assured today will be no exception.'

'I don't know who you are, but you should give yourself up while you have the chance. I have armed men entering the building as we speak. Walk down the stairs and enter the lobby with your hands placed behind your head.'

'Inspector, please. Raised voices are not part of the Tribeca ethos. We are so very happy you were able to join us here today. As with all Tribeca guests, you should want for nothing during your stay. If there is anything you need, please don't hesitate to contact me personally.'

Unable to control his growing anger, Savage's voice continued to rise. 'I want you to know the hotel is being placed into lockdown. There will be no way in and no way out,' he shouted. 'We will search the building floor by floor until we have you cornered. You should take the opportunity to give yourself up while you can.'

But the voice on the phone remained calm. 'As hotel manager, I have to say how sorry I am Jackson Harlington had to cut short his stay. The last thing we ever want is a dissatisfied guest. Hopefully we went some way towards making his stay a memorable one.'

There was a pause.

'And Inspector, please do be assured you'll be hearing from me again once you've had a chance to fully settle in and acquaint yourself with our luxurious surroundings. I like to ensure as many of our guests as possible receive my own very special attention.'

CHAPTER 9

ROSCOE WATCHED as Savage slammed down the phone before turning to face him.

'We're dealing with a madman. He's completely insane.'

'Any specific demands?'

'Nothing. We're not going to be able to negotiate. He thinks he's running the hotel. Said he hoped I would enjoy my stay. Total nut job. We've got to close this place down, no one in, no one out. In the end he'll be left with nowhere to hide.'

But Roscoe was concerned at the thought of keeping over a hundred people trapped in the hotel.

'I think you're wrong. We need to start getting these people out of here. They're not safe. Any one of them could be the next target.' He softened his tone, remembering the best way to get Savage on side was to flatter his oversized ego. 'Peter, nobody can run this kind of operation the way you can. You've already established a dialogue. Wherever he was phoning from we know it wasn't this lobby, which means it's safe for you to make the call and start getting people evacuated.'

'That always was your problem – looking for the easy option,' said Savage. 'Any one of these people could be involved. They might even be working in conjunction with our man on the phone.

'I see it like this,' he explained. 'Our man kills Harlington on the thirty-eighth floor. Next thing we know, he's stabbing your guy on the fourth floor. That sounds to me like he moves pretty quick. Who's to say we aren't dealing with more than one madman here? You've got to learn to take these things one step at a time, Roscoe. Slowly, slowly, catchee monkey – that's the way to do things.'

He turned away from Roscoe to repeat his instruction that nobody was to enter or leave the building without his personal say-so.

Roscoe took a deep breath to control his anger.

'Peter, this is a siege. We should be getting these people out of here. This isn't a time for slowly, slowly.'

Savage walked across to Roscoe and leant into him.

'I'm not going to argue about this. At the very least these people are witnesses. Why would I let them walk outside to do a string of media interviews? Any one of them could be linked to Jackson Harlington's murder. A business deal gone bad? He was a rich man, wasn't he? Any one of these folk could have come here for revenge.' He paused and looked around the lobby. 'Nobody leaves this building.'

'I can't listen to you any more,' said Roscoe, stepping away. But Savage refused to let him go.

'When I say anyone here could have been involved, Roscoe, I'm including you. Any kind of security in this place to begin with, and I wouldn't need to be here now to clean up your mess.'

Roscoe's long-running disdain for the inspector boiled suddenly to the surface. Turning quickly, he shaped to hit him. But before he had the chance to throw his punch, Anna stepped in, taking hold of his arm, telling him Savage wasn't worth it. Roscoe watched Savage smirk, knowing he had let the serving officer get under his skin.

'Let me ask you this, Savage,' Roscoe said, leaning in towards his former colleague. 'Do you have any idea how many ways there are in and out of this building? No? I can tell you. There are sixteen. You've got what, six, eight men? You can't hope to secure a building of this size. We need to act now or Jackson Harlington's killer will be gone.'

Savage stepped back, intimidated as much by Roscoe's superior thinking as by his superior physique.

'Trust me, Roscoe, he's still here. I spoke to him. I'm telling you, he's going nowhere. And neither are you.'

Roscoe accepted that the one thing Savage was probably right about was the fact the killer was still in the hotel. It was impossible to know where, but after stabbing Stanley he had made his choice to stay in the building.

He looked across as the paramedics lifted Stanley onto a stretcher and prepared to wheel him out of the building. He turned to Savage.

'Peter, this man needs to get to a hospital,' he said. 'If he's to have any hope of recovery he can't be held here a second longer.'

Savage stared at Roscoe, bringing his hand to his mouth but saying nothing.

Roscoe moved closer to him.

'I said no one was to leave,' repeated Savage.

Another inch forward.

'But okay, I'll make an exception,' said Savage. 'He can go,' he told the paramedics.

'Thank you,' spat Roscoe. 'Always so humane.'

'Don't thank me, Roscoe. Your man looks like he'll be dead by the time he reaches the emergency room.'

Roscoe ignored Savage and ran towards the exit, stopping the paramedics before they wheeled Stanley out of the building.

'Hang in there, Stanley,' he said. 'You're going to be okay, I know you are.'

Stanley opened his eyes.

'You get him, boss. Get him for me.'

'Don't worry, I will.' And before Roscoe could say any more the paramedics pushed Stanley through the door and out to the waiting ambulance.

From inside the lobby, Roscoe watched them carefully load him in the emergency vehicle before repeating to himself, 'Don't worry, Stanley, I will. Whatever it takes.'

CHAPTER 10

JON ROSCOE STOOD at the cathedral-like windows which poured light onto the marbled lobby of the Tribeca Luxury Hotel. He felt a physical pain as the ambulance accelerated away, lighting up its sirens as it went.

'Where do I go next, Stanley?' he asked himself.

'He wanted to speak to us,' he told himself, paging through the events of the last hour in his head. 'He wanted to talk to whoever was in charge, wanted to taunt us, to show us he was in control. He might be crazy but he knows what he's doing. And he's not done yet, Stanley. But where is he? Where was he calling from? We know he must have been in the hotel.

'Of course!' he called out, causing those around him to turn and stare. He sprinted across the lobby. 'Anna! Anna! Can you tell where he was calling from? The killer?'

Anna picked up the phone on her desk and clicked through the calls she'd received.

'An internal phone on the twenty-fifth floor.'

'You're certain?'

'Absolutely. This gives me a floor-by-floor breakdown.'

'Can you see what room?'

'It was a hallway phone.'

'So why the twenty-fifth? What's taken him there?' Roscoe stood beside Anna's desk while she clicked on her computer.

She turned to him, a look of dread on her face.

'Jon, twenty-five – it's where Jackson Harlington's family are staying. The Royal Garden Suite.'

'Damn him,' said Roscoe, hitting out at the wall behind Anna's desk. 'He's a step ahead of us. Why didn't I bring them straight down to the lobby?'

He handed Anna his security pass. 'If you enter my details you'll be able to access the cameras on twenty-five.'

Roscoe leant across to Anna's desk as she typed in his passcode. In a split second an image of the hallway on the twenty-fifth floor appeared on Anna's monitor. He flicked from one camera image to the next but all they could see was silence.

The hallway was deserted.

Nothing was out of place.

Roscoe took in a sharp breath. 'I've got to get up there.'

Neither Roscoe nor Anna Conquest had noticed the approach of Peter Savage as they viewed the images.

'Get up where?' demanded Savage.

Roscoe said nothing.

'Perhaps you'd like to be the one who shares, Ms Conquest?'

Anna looked up at Jon. He knew this wasn't her battle to fight.

'The twenty-fifth floor,' said Roscoe. 'We think it's where he was calling from. And we know it's where the Harlington family are staying.'

'And you thought it was smart to keep that to yourself, did you, Rambo? This is a police investigation, not an opportunity for hotel security to play detective. I'll take an armed unit up in the elevator. Roscoe, you can stay here and answer the phones.'

Savage called across two armed officers and quickly briefed them with a plan to access the twenty-fifth floor. The elevators would be unlocked and he would travel with them in the express elevator. On reaching the hallway, they would secure the space before accessing the three separate suites that covered the floor. They would start with the Royal Garden Suite, where Jackson Harlington had been staying with his wife and daughter.

Savage turned to Roscoe.

'Unlock the elevators.'

Realising he had no choice, Roscoe walked across the lobby and keyed in the security code. Savage pressed the button to call the express elevator but as soon as he did the neighbouring elevator began a descent from the twenty-fifth floor.

Roscoe was the first to react.

Seeing the elevator drop floor by floor, he shouted across the lobby.

'Everyone get back now! Take whatever cover you can!' He backed away from the elevator doors, pushing his arms forward to move people away. 'Take cover behind whatever you can. Get back! Now!'

He ran back across the lobby, watching the elevator continue its relentless descent. His heart pounding, he knew every life was in imminent danger.

'Do you think it's him, Roscoe?' asked Savage, appearing fearful as he struggled to act in the immediate face of danger.

'I don't know, but we need to get everyone as far away from the elevator doors as possible.'

'Back!' yelled Savage, following Roscoe's lead.

Roscoe watched as the floors ticked past.

Nineteen, eighteen, seventeen.

'We need to be ready for him, Peter,' said Roscoe.

Savage deployed three armed officers at the elevator doors. Crouching down, each officer released the safety catches on their semi-automatic weapons.

Fourteen, thirteen, twelve.

Savage reached across and handed a Glock 26 to Roscoe.

'You know how to use this better than anyone.'

Roscoe knelt directly in front of the elevator doors. He would be the first to fire.

Ten, nine, eight.

Standing behind his officers, Savage pulled his own weapon. The foyer was silent, all eyes fixed on the elevator countdown.

Five, four, three, two, one.

Lobby.

CHAPTER 11

ROSCOE'S FINGER TIGHTENED on the trigger.

Sweat ran down Peter Savage's back.

Everyone across the marble lobby held a breath.

And the elevator doors opened.

Silence.

Inside, an office chair was slowly spinning to a halt.

Roscoe's finger twitched on the trigger as the chair made its final turn to face forward.

Screams.

The mutilated naked body of a middle-aged man was exposed to all. The body was bound to the chair by a leather belt, his chest cracked open and his heart ripped to the surface.

At the sight of the blood-soaked body, Savage heaved and turned away. Unable to look upon the obliterated body, he walked away from the elevator. Breathing deeply, he tried to fill his lungs and to regain his composure.

Roscoe slowly lowered his weapon. The floor of the elevator was soaked in the man's blood. He stepped forward to the edge of the door and saw the dead man was holding a sign written in blood:

'HOTEL UNDER NEW MANAGEMENT.'

Behind him, Roscoe heard screams continue from the shocked onlookers as he very carefully lifted the dead man's head to try to identify him. Immediately he recognised the man as Michael Duncan, one of the hotel's specialist security drivers. Roscoe had appointed him the previous week on the personal recommendation of Jackson Harlington. Duncan had been detailed to bring Harlington's business partner, Oscar Miller, to the hotel earlier in the day.

Roscoe walked back from the elevator and indicated to the three armed police officers to disengage their weapons. He looked across at Savage and saw he was still shaking.

Knowing he was being watched, Savage forced himself to take a hesitant step towards Roscoe. Breathing heavily, he attempted again to regain his composure.

'What kind of man are we dealing with, Roscoe?' asked Savage, failing to hide the tremble in his voice. 'I've never seen anything like this. What has he done to him?'

Savage became hypnotised by the sight of the dead man's body, unable to draw his eyes away from the shattered chest and eviscerated heart.

'Is that his heart?' he asked, unable to comprehend what he was seeing. 'My God, Jon, he's an executioner.'

'Look at me, Peter,' ordered Roscoe, stepping across to Savage, putting his arm around his shoulder and steering him away from the elevator. 'This is brutal, but you're the officer in charge and you have to show it.'

'I can't, Jon. Look what he's done. He's some kind of animal. Insane.' Roscoe could hear the panic rising in Savage's voice.

'If the body's come down from the twenty-fifth floor, it means the Harlington family are in danger. We need to get upstairs and find them. You need to lead your team and we need to stop this man before he kills again.'

Savage took a deep breath.

'You're right. We can do this,' he said, reassuring himself. 'You and I, we can do this. We were a good team when we worked together. Good cop, bad cop – in every sense of the word.'

Roscoe offered a smile in an attempt to support his former colleague. Savage was right. This was a brutal attack, not something he had ever seen the like of before. And he knew they had to go to the Harlington family – whatever it meant they might discover. 'We need to go upstairs now. We've got to go to twenty-five.'

Savage called over two of the armed officers to accompany them up the building, leaving one officer to secure the scene.

In silence they walked past the blood-soaked elevator, Roscoe pressing the call button for the neighbouring one. As the doors opened, the three men and one woman stepped inside.

Journeying up through the building, Roscoe wondered what might greet them on the twenty-fifth floor. When the elevator doors finally opened, he led them out onto the hallway's hand-woven Indian rug, weapon drawn. As he did so, he heard a desperate cry for help.

It was coming from the Royal Garden Suite.

CHAPTER 12

QUICKLY AND WITHOUT HESITATION, Roscoe moved down the hallway, his position covered by the armed officers following close behind him. As he reached the door to the Royal Garden Suite, another terrified cry for help came from inside the room. He pushed at the door but found it securely locked. He reached for his access pass, only to realise he had left it with Anna. Immediately he grabbed a fire extinguisher from the hall, smashed the lock and then forced the door open.

The living room and dining room were both deserted. Roscoe crossed to the entrance to the main bedroom and indicated to one of the officers to open the door as he and Savage covered him.

Another piercing scream came from inside the room.

The door swung open.

Roscoe turned to Savage and quietly said, 'Thank God for that.'

Tied back to back on the bed were Jacqueline Harlington, the daughter of Jackson Harlington, and Oscar Miller. Miller had been struck on the head and blood had run down across his face. Both he and Jacqueline had been gagged but Jacqueline had worked her gag loose, making her the source of the cries for help. The police officers scanned the room as Roscoe pointed towards the closed bathroom door.

'My mom's in the bathroom,' Jacqueline Harlington sobbed. 'Be quick. You need to see if she's okay.'

Roscoe ran to the bathroom and threw open the door. Lying on the floor was Jocasta Harlington, her hands tied, her feet bound and a gag tightly wrapped around her mouth. Roscoe knelt on the bathroom floor, removing the gag and untying the ropes, which he saw had cut into her wrists.

'Jacqueline?' came the first cry from Jocasta.

'It's okay, Mom, I'm here. I'm okay.'

'And Oscar?'

'I'll be fine,' replied Oscar Miller, a little blearily but with nothing more than superficial injuries.

'Thank you, God,' cried Jocasta. 'And thank you, Jon,' she said, turning to Roscoe, the man who had headed her husband's security team for the past two years.

'Can you tell me what happened, Mrs Harlington?' asked Roscoe.

He helped Jocasta to her feet and supported her as she walked shakily into the bedroom. Jacqueline and Oscar Miller had been untied by the officers and Jocasta rushed across to hug her daughter.

'I can see this has been a horrible ordeal, Mrs Harlington,' persisted Roscoe, 'but we need to know what happened.'

'Jon, it was terrifying – horrendous. Jackson had invited Oscar to come up to the suite when he was ready.' Jocasta suddenly stopped and turned to the police officers. 'Jackson?' she exclaimed. 'Where's Jackson? Jon, he took Jackson. Where's my husband?'

Stepping forward, Roscoe sat on the corner of the bed next to Jocasta and her daughter. 'It's not good, Mrs Harlington,' he said.

Jocasta's eyes filled with tears. 'He's dead, isn't he?' she asked, as Roscoe wondered if she already knew the answer she was about to receive.

'I'm afraid so,' he said, putting his hand on her arm.

Jacqueline Harlington let out a cry at the news of the death of her father as Oscar Miller put his hand to his face. Jocasta Harlington sat motionless and somehow retained her composure.

'I think I knew,' she said. 'The man was heavily armed. When Jackson opened the door to welcome Oscar, he easily forced his way in. As soon as he was in the room he hit

Jackson across the head, knocked him unconscious with the butt of his gun. Jackson went straight down.' Jacqueline started to sob as her mother continued, 'He wore a mask the whole time. A ski mask, I think. He threatened to shoot us all, Jon. Jackson was on the floor, hardly moving. He tied up Oscar and Jacqueline. Oscar started to struggle.'

Jocasta turned to Oscar Miller. 'Why did you do that, Oscar? He might have killed you.' Only now did she show any real emotion. 'He struck Oscar and then he dragged me into the bathroom. I thought he was going to kill me but all he did was tie me up. He left me lying on the floor and I could see him going back to Jackson. Jackson was coming round and he dragged him to his feet. I started screaming and that's when he came back in and gagged me. Then he closed the door and left me. After that I didn't see any more.'

She bowed her head and Roscoe could see the physical effort she had to make to stop herself breaking down, as her hands trembled on her knees.

'Thank you, Mrs Harlington,' he said before turning to Jacqueline. 'I know this is difficult, but can you tell me what happened after that?' he asked her.

'He came back out, grabbed hold of my father, pointed the gun at his head and forced him out of the room. And that was it until you came in,' said Jacqueline, wiping the tears from her eyes.

'How long since he left?'

'It feels like hours, Jon, but I'm guessing it's no more than thirty or forty minutes,' Jocasta said.

Roscoe turned to Savage. 'He's working to a timetable,' he said quietly. 'When he called us from the twenty-fifth floor he knew we'd head upstairs. He was waiting for us to unlock the elevators and as soon as we did he sent down his message. By the time we get up here, he's long gone.'

'Did any of you recognise him at all?' asked Savage. 'Or feel like you knew him or might have known him in any way?'

'He wore the mask,' said Jacqueline. 'There was no way we would've been able to recognise him even if we did know him.'

'What about his voice?' pressed Savage. 'Anything at all that struck a chord with you?'

'He never spoke,' said Jacqueline. 'Not a word. Nothing.'

'What about you, Mrs Harlington. Any recognition?' continued Savage. 'Anything you might be able to tell us could be vital.'

'I'm sorry, no. I wish there was. We've told you everything.'

'Can you tell us what happened to my father?' asked Jacqueline Harlington, looking directly at Savage.

Savage couldn't answer. He turned to Roscoe for help. Silence hung in the air.

'I'm sorry, Miss Harlington. It seems like the hotel is, I don't know . . .' said Roscoe, struggling for words, 'it seems as if the hotel is under some kind of attack. I'm afraid Mr Harlington was killed as part of that. Right now we've every reason to believe the killer is still in the hotel, and that means we need to get you somewhere safe.'

'We should take you downstairs, Mrs Harlington. All of you. We can get medical attention for Mr Miller,' added Savage.

The police officers started to help Jocasta Harlington and her daughter to their feet.

'Savage,' said Roscoe softly. 'He could have killed all three of them if he'd wanted to. But he chose not to. He killed Jackson Harlington and Michael Duncan but he didn't kill Harlington's wife, daughter or business partner. I'm telling you – this is something personal.'

Roscoe could see Savage didn't want to get into a discussion around the killer's motive.

'Let's get these people downstairs,' said Savage sharply, 'and then maybe we start a general evacuation. You were right, Jon. We've got to get everyone out before it's too late.'

And then the phone in the suite started to ring.

CHAPTER 13

IN THE ROYAL GARDEN SUITE, the phone continued to ring loudly.

Roscoe looked across at Savage and saw a man frozen with fear.

The phone continued to ring.

All eyes in the room turned towards the inspector, who stood motionless.

The phone continued to ring.

Seeing that Savage was petrified, Roscoe stepped forward. 'He's already spoken to you, Peter. You're the one who can build a relationship with him. Answer it.'

'No,' said Savage as his eyes rapidly raced around the room. 'It should be you, Jon,' he insisted, desperately searching for a reason as to why.

The phone continued to ring.

'I've spoken to him once. I think it would be good for you to build an understanding of him as well,' said Savage.

Roscoe watched him trying to convince himself as much as anyone else in the room.

Roscoe grabbed the phone. 'This is Jon Roscoe.'

'No Inspector Savage? Now that is disappointing. Perhaps he is enjoying the wealth of amenities we offer to all our valued guests here at Tribeca Luxury Hotels.'

'Perhaps.'

'And so, Jon Roscoe, what is it you do?'

'I head up security here at the hotel.'

'Oh dear. I think we might need to have a meeting, Jon Roscoe, as from what I understand, things aren't going too well on that front.'

'This needs to stop,' said Roscoe. 'And it needs to stop now!'

'I take it you've freed my hostages on the twenty-fifth floor.'

'We're helping Mrs Harlington and her daughter, yes. And Mr Miller.'

The killer was silent.

'Tell me, what are you trying to achieve?' said Roscoe.

'I think we all want the same thing – for the grand opening of the Tribeca Luxury Hotel in London's Mayfair to be remembered around the world for a very long time.'

'I think you might have achieved that already,' Roscoe said, determined to keep the killer talking.

'As you say, Jon Roscoe, perhaps.'

'So what now?'

'Didn't I say? How remiss of me. Not the level of service we expect here at Tribeca. Allow me to apologise. As the new manager of the hotel I've given instructions for a very special lunch to be prepared. I do hope you enjoy it.'

The phone went dead.

'That's it, he's disconnected,' said Roscoe, turning to the room.

Savage moved forward in an attempt to assert control. 'I should head for the kitchen. That's where he wants us to go.'

'Exactly,' warned Roscoe. 'That's what he wants. He's always a step ahead of us. His next move is for us all to charge down to the kitchen. Let's not fall into that trap. I say we get everyone in here safe and when that's done we secure the area around the kitchen and the restaurant. If we throw our net wide enough, we'll have him trapped.'

CHAPTER 14

HAVING LIVED IN LONDON all of her life, Jessie Luck knew her way around every one of the city's winding backstreets. With traffic as bad as ever, she drove herself around the side streets of Mayfair, avoiding all the main roads and congestion. Pulling up to the rear of the Tribeca Luxury Hotel, she stopped in the employee parking lot and made her way to the kitchen entrance of the hotel.

Jessie was surprised to find the hotel so deserted but didn't give it a second thought. She knew everyone would be busy throughout the building in preparation for the grand opening later in the week. She went to buzz the kitchen intercom, but saw the figure of a man by the main kitchen entrance and quickly made her way over to him.

'Hello,' Jessie called to him. The door was open, and he was standing just inside. 'I was hoping you might be able to give me a hand. At my age I can still manage to do the baking but my days of carrying in the boxes are long gone.

There's a muffin in it for you if you can help me,' she smiled at him.

There was no response, so Jessie guessed the man hadn't heard her.

'Hello,' she called again. 'Hello, I wondered if you might be able to help me?'

She saw the figure step back inside the kitchen. Never one to be deterred, she followed. Entering the vast room, with row upon row of stainless steel preparation benches and tables, she saw the figure turn away from her and move to the back of the kitchen.

Beginning to feel slightly irate at being ignored, she called out again in a voice designed to show her growing displeasure, 'Excuse me, I wondered if you might be able to give me a hand. I've a number of boxes— '

Jessie stopped.

The figure turned and walked slowly towards her.

For the first time she saw that the man was wearing a black ski mask to hide his face, but that almost didn't register with her.

The man was covered in blood.

His arms hung by his sides and in one hand he was carrying a decapitated human head. The head was rotating from side to side as he gripped it by the hair on its scalp.

Jessie stood open-mouthed, staring at the man, but refused to run away. The man stopped moving towards her.

Standing in front of the open door, Jessie realised she was blocking his route of escape. She edged to one side. At any moment he might come at her. He could probably kill her with one blow yet at that moment she didn't feel afraid.

'I guess you won't be helping me with my boxes, but perhaps I can help you?' she said, surprising herself at her calm approach. 'Why don't I stand to the side? Or maybe I should walk away from you, out into the parking lot?'

For a split second Jessie thought the man might respond, but before she could say any more he had dropped the head onto the spotlessly clean floor, leapt onto one of the benches and then jumped across the room from one bench to the next. At the back of the kitchen he vaulted off the final bench, ran towards the service elevator, and before Jessie knew it he was gone.

Jessie looked at the kitchen. She could see the abandoned head lying on the floor, blood splattered around it. Towards the back of the room she could see a blood-soaked bench. There was a body lying on top of it. In the silence of the kitchen she could hear a steady drip of blood onto the polished floor.

She turned to the kitchen exit and suddenly found herself screaming for Jon.

CHAPTER 15

ROSCOE COULD STILL REMEMBER the very first time he tasted a home-baked cake, made with Jessie's secret ingredients of love and kindness, in the tiny kitchen of her small apartment in the Brixton area of London. It was his third birthday and from that day forward he'd known nobody could bake cakes the way his aunt Jessie could.

Jessie had lived in the apartment upstairs from the Roscoe family and it hadn't taken her long to realise Jon's dad was a bad lot. She'd been able to hear the shouting each evening when Colin Roscoe returned home and Jessie had increasingly feared for Jon and his mother. While never one to shy away from confrontation, she'd known the best thing she could do to help was not enrage Colin Roscoe any further. Jessie had started to call in each morning and afternoon to make sure Helen Roscoe was coping and she had everything she needed for her young son. She'd known not to insult Helen by offering her money, but she'd had a special skill at finding whatever it was Helen or Jon needed at any point in time, usually hidden away in her old wardrobe or tucked away at the back of her kitchen cupboard. She'd loved how Jon had begun to think of her wardrobe as a magical place, and had known Helen never ceased to be grateful for the toys or clothes or bikes which Jessie had found, having kept them since her own teenage son, Alvin, was a small boy.

The one time Jessie had offered Helen money was the day Colin Roscoe had left for good. She'd known he was gone for ever, and although she'd been relieved for Helen, she had known that while he'd been a bad lot, Colin had at least provided a roof over his family's heads. Now Helen was alone in the world – her, her son and her unborn child.

Jessie hadn't had a huge amount herself, but when Alvin's father had died two years before he had left her and their son enough to live on. She'd gone to Helen with her first month's rent and had received a promise it would be repaid as soon as Helen received her first paycheque from the two jobs she had taken on. Jessie had insisted there was no need, but the day after Helen had been paid, the loan amount had been quietly slipped under Jessie's front door. Jessie had known to accept the money graciously, but in the weeks that followed, some extra discoveries would be made at the back of her magic wardrobe.

Jessie and Helen had become the closest of friends, and to Jon, Aunt Jessie had become a second mother. On the nights his mum would be working, Jon would go upstairs for his supper and then Jessie would love putting him down to sleep in her own bed. When Helen would come home from work, she'd wrap Jon in a blanket and carefully carry him down the stairs, before handing him over to his mother's waiting arms. Every night when Helen took hold of her son, Jessie's heart would break as she saw how close to exhaustion her dear friend had become.

Jessie often thought of the day Jon's baby sister, Amanda, arrived in the world – arriving in great haste on a cold and wet December evening. Helen had stopped working the week before and with Jon safely asleep in bed, she'd sat watching television with Jessie. As Jessie had cleared away the dinner plates, and Alvin had finished his homework, Helen had rested her feet in front of the latest soap opera. Very quickly, all of the action had been in Jessie's apartment and with the baby on her way, Jessie had called a cab to take her and Helen to the hospital while Alvin was given clear instructions on what he needed to do to care for Jon. But Alvin had known that part would be easy. Jon had idolised Alvin, loving him like a big brother, and would always behave whenever he asked him to.

Jessie had helped Helen into the cab, but as they'd made their way through the London streets they'd got caught up in the traffic created by eager Christmas shoppers. Jessie had praised the Lord as the cab driver had performed miracles to get them to the hospital in double-quick time but the real miracle had been in the back of the cab, where she'd delivered Helen's baby daughter. When the cab had arrived at the hospital the cord had been cut and Helen's new baby had been carried into the building. Helen and Jessie had followed along with two nurses and it hadn't been long before Helen was sitting up in bed nursing baby Amanda Jessica. Jessie had smiled the broadest smile and felt for the first time that her family was complete.

Jessie had known life for Helen was never going to be easy with two young children and two jobs but she had been happy doing everything she could to help. Often in the evening she would see Helen arrive home exhausted as she made her way downstairs to carefully hand over both of the children. Over time, she'd seen the sparkle disappear from Helen; her smiles were gone and the laughter in her eyes, which had appeared after Colin had left, had gradually faded away.

On a warm summer evening, Jessie had sat with Helen in their small, shared garden and had told her friend she looked shattered. Tears had welled in Jessie's eyes as Helen broke down and admitted she was finding life harder and harder. Jessie had suggested they take the children away for the weekend, and two weeks later they'd been walking in sun-drenched open fields. Jessie had known it had been the right thing to do as Jon had run across the fields with Alvin while Amanda had toddled along, holding hands with Helen and Jessie. After two wonderful days, they'd caught the bus back to London and home.

As the bus had pulled into Victoria station, Jessie had seen that Helen had fallen asleep and she'd reached across to wake her. But she hadn't been able to stir her dearest friend and suddenly Jessie had been standing with the three children, watching Helen being loaded into the back of an ambulance. Twenty-four hours later, Helen's diagnosis had been made. The cancer had spread to her bones and suddenly she'd had to decide about the future of her children. Tears had filled her eyes as Helen had asked Jessie to take care of Jon and Amanda after she was gone. Jessie hadn't hesitated for a moment and when the time had come, Jon and Amanda had made their way up the stairs and Jessie's home had become theirs.

Jessie still remembered the first night when Jon had moved into her home, how he and Alvin had carried his toys up the stairs, and how as he'd walked into the apartment, he had smelt the most delicious cakes she had spent the afternoon baking. On his saddest day, as he'd sat at her kitchen table and eaten his way through three chocolate muffins, she had been able to see that he was beginning to feel warm inside. Amanda had been sitting next to him, and Jessie had been able to see how protective Jon felt of his little sister.

Two years later, Jessie had adopted Jon and Amanda and Aunt Jessie became the only real mother Amanda could remember. Jon had still thought of his own mother, but Jessie had known that he loved her as much as any child could love a mother.

Throughout Jon's childhood, Jessie would spend every Saturday baking fresh cakes and brownies for her family and creating her own most wonderful recipes. When the coffee shop folk had moved into Brixton, suddenly cakes and baking had become cool. Jessie had listened to Jon's encouragement and now she had her own successful business. And with Jon working at the new London Tribeca Hotel, it seemed only right that Auntie's Bakery would be the supplier of the best home-cooked muffins and doughnuts anywhere in London.

CHAPTER 16

JESSIE RAN THROUGH THE KITCHEN and into the majestic dining room, where in three days' time some of the wealthiest and most influential clientele were due to be served the best food a hotel restaurant had ever presented. But as she moved through the restaurant, she realised it was stupid of her to be screaming for Jon. The hotel was vast and he could be anywhere on one of its forty floors. If only he were there right now, she thought in desperation.

And then he was.

Seeing him entering the dining room, she kept running, as fast as she possibly could, until she reached him.

'Jon,' she cried, running into his arms. And then he was holding her as tight as she had used to hold him.

'Aunt Jessie?' he said, hugging her and almost forgetting what had gone before. 'Where did you come from?'

She looked up at him, the thoughtful boy she'd raised and now the strong, brave man she adored. Looking at his handsome face, she knew she had to tell him what she had seen, however horrendous it was.

'I was in the kitchen, Jon,' she cried, starting to shake. 'It . . . It was horrible. Horrible!'

'It's okay, Aunt Jessie. I'm here now. You're safe. What did you see?'

'A head, Jon. A human head. Cut off from its body. There's a head in the kitchen.'

'No, Aunt Jessie,' said Roscoe, holding her closely to his chest. 'I'm sorry. I'm so sorry you had to see that.'

Jessie looked up at the man she loved as a son and only then realised he had a gun in his hand.

She stepped back.

'Jon? What's happening?'

'The hotel is under attack. I think it's probably by just one man, but from what you're telling me that's the third person he's killed today.' Roscoe paused. 'I've got to ask you this – but where was the head?' he said, not wanting to upset his aunt any further but knowing he needed to find the killer.

'Jon, he was holding it!' yelled Aunt Jessie, burying her head further into Jon's chest. 'And then he dropped it onto the floor.'

Holding tightly on to his aunt, Roscoe realised she had come face to face with the killer. He couldn't imagine the unspeakable horror she had seen in the kitchen. After a moment, he stepped slightly away to look into Aunt Jessie's tear-filled eyes.

'Did you see his face?' he asked, still holding her hands but stepping backwards in the direction of the kitchen.

'No, he was wearing a mask.'

'And he's still in there now?' said Roscoe, letting go of her and starting to walk through the vaulted dining room to the kitchen.

'He scrambled over the kitchen tables and I think he went into the elevator. But where are you going?'

'Aunt Jessie, how did you get into the hotel?'

'Through the kitchen door. I saw him in the doorway and followed him inside.'

'Aunt Jessie,' said Roscoe as he approached the kitchen door, his gun still drawn, 'I want you to go straight through those doors at the front of the restaurant and down the hall-way to the lobby. Find Anna. She'll be somewhere there. She'll look after you. The police are evacuating the hotel and you'll be able to leave through the front with her.'

'But what about you, Jon?' asked Jessie, looking lovingly at him.

'I know you don't like it, Aunt Jessie, but it's my job. Right now I have to try to catch a killer.'

CHAPTER 17

IN FIFTEEN YEARS of working for London's Metropolitan Police, Jon Roscoe had seen some horrific sights. He'd been witness to explosions, arrived first on scene after the discovery of decaying bodies hauled from London's River Thames, and had had his emotions drained as the first responder to cases of domestic abuse. But nothing prepared him for the discovery he found in the new kitchens of the London Tribeca Luxury Hotel.

He entered through the front of the kitchen and slowly worked his way past each kitchen bench. With his weapon drawn, he anticipated the killer appearing at any moment. Slowly making his way to the back wall, he discovered the desperate scene where the killer had carried out his work. Laid across the stainless steel kitchen work surface was the decapitated body of one of the hotel chefs, his white chef's jacket turned red with his own blood.

The killer had scythed through his victim's neck.

Blood still dripped from the corpse. As with Jackson Harlington and Michael Duncan, the killer had ripped through his victim's chest and torn his heart from its cavity.

Two benches to the right, discarded on the floor, was the victim's head. The dead man's startled eyes stared up at Roscoe and for a moment he had to turn away from a discovery he found genuinely shocking.

Turning back, he stepped towards the mangled corpse. Breathing deeply, he leant over the body to see if there was any way of making an identification. Still pinned to the victim's chest was his Tribeca Luxury Hotels name badge and pass. Richard Winn was a pastry chef in the kitchen but not someone Roscoe had ever met. He would ask Anna to pull his employment records.

The kitchen at the London Tribeca Luxury Hotel is designed to give direct access to all of the guest floors. Each of the suites has their own luxury kitchen and chef, but the main kitchen is designed to service all areas of the hotel, twenty-four hours a day. Roscoe looked at the service elevator, intended to deliver the finest cuisine to any guest at a moment's notice. It was still making its deathly climb through the hotel. Where was the killer heading next in this seemingly endless brutal game of chase around the building? And what could be the motive for such vicious attacks?

Roscoe had seen men and woman kill and be killed. He had seen rage, fear, greed and passion, but the act of killing was almost always their last act. With this killer, such was the fury, the killing alone was not enough: the death had to be brutal, the corpse mutilated. These were some of the most horrific deaths Roscoe had seen in his career. He thought that if he could comprehend what was behind such violence, he might be able to understand what was driving the killer, and what he planned next. And these weren't random killings: Roscoe could see everything had been meticulously planned. His passage around the hotel had been carefully plotted. He was certain the killer had already decided exactly what his next move would be.

Counting off each luxury floor of the hotel, Roscoe saw the service elevator had reached its final destination. The fortieth floor.

He crossed the kitchen and stood at the open door Aunt Jessie had come through. He thought how less than twenty-four hours before, he had explored the top floor of the hotel. Standing on the glass-floored terrace, looking over the sparkling water flowing from the infinity pool, he and Stanley had marvelled at the latest addition to the Tribeca Luxury Hotel collection. They had walked all the public spaces in preparation for today's preview of the hotel. Had they missed something? Had they both been so taken with the brilliance of the hotel they'd become distracted from its security? Roscoe knew that somehow somebody had gained access to the secure areas of the hotel, which had allowed him to cause devastation beyond belief and had left Stanley's life hanging in the balance. He told himself he'd even put Aunt Jessie in danger. How had he let that happen? He was here to protect people, especially those he loved.

In his mind, he retraced his steps through the hotel. He was certain he hadn't missed anything. The hotel had been secure ahead of the opening. There was no way for someone to gain such unlimited access around the hotel – but this man had. How had he found his way to Jackson Harlington's suite? How did he have such an in-depth knowledge of the hotel? And what was driving him?

To kill Jackson Harlington in such a sacrificial manner could only have been caused by absolute hatred of the man. But what of Michael Duncan, and now Richard Winn? Were the three deaths linked? Roscoe was convinced they had to be. But he needed to be absolutely certain; he needed to speak to Anna Conquest.

Stepping back into the kitchen and closing the open door, Roscoe felt the killer was ready to play out his final performance. He had made his way to the summit of the hotel, and Roscoe was convinced that was where he would finally meet him.

CHAPTER 18

IN THE LOBBY of the hotel, Inspector Savage was beginning the evacuation. He knew the dangers of evacuating over a hundred people through the front of the hotel, and how they would represent an open target for anyone in the hotel intent on carrying out further random killings. But Savage knew these killings weren't random.

Jackson Harlington had been a target.

Michael Dunn had been a target.

Savage had police marksmen positioned outside the front of the hotel, with instructions to open fire if the killer showed himself. Snipers were ready to take him down if he appeared on any one of the hotel's forty floors. A plan had been established, with all of the evacuees issued with clear instructions. The front entrance of the hotel would be opened. Exit would be in single file with a right turn created twenty yards into the garden, leading to a neighbouring property. Within the neighbouring property a safe area had been established where witnesses would be questioned and statements taken.

Police protocol would be followed. Savage knew it was the right thing to do. Except he also knew police protocol wouldn't catch this killer. The only way this could end was with a bullet through the killer's heart.

Roscoe ran back into the lobby, where he saw Anna Conquest crouching beside a chair as she comforted Aunt Jessie. Jessie had clearly been shocked by what she'd witnessed but Roscoe didn't know anybody with a stronger resolve than his aunt Jessie. He went straight to them, but as he did, Peter Savage came across the lobby to join them.

'What's going on, Roscoe? This old woman says there has been another killing?'

Roscoe ignored Savage and turned to his aunt. 'You remember me telling you about Inspector Savage, Aunt Jessie? Well, allow me to introduce you.'

Jessie sniffed in disgust. 'I guessed as much, Jon. You always said what a little shit he was.'

Anna Conquest couldn't help laughing.

Roscoe smiled at Aunt Jessie. 'That might well be the case, but Inspector Savage is heading up the police operation.'

'I can tell you this, Inspector Savage,' said Jessie, looking the police officer directly in the eye, 'this old woman wouldn't say there had been another killing if she hadn't seen one. And what she saw was a killer holding a dead man's head in his hand.'

Savage turned to Roscoe, who nodded. 'The body's in the kitchen,' he said. 'It's brutal.'

'We have to get him, Roscoe,' said Savage, looking more determined than he'd been since arriving at the hotel. 'We have to get him. I don't care how. We have to take him down.'

Roscoe turned to Anna. 'Can you access the hotel personnel records?'

'I can do it from here,' replied Anna, moving back to her desk. 'What do you need to know?'

'When we hired Richard Winn and anything else we have on him.'

'No problem.'

'Richard Winn?' asked Savage. 'Where does he fit in?'

'Our latest victim,' said Roscoe. 'The killer might have obliterated his body but his security badge was left intact – for what that's worth.'

Savage turned away from the group, as if he was planning what he should do next. The killings were getting more violent, if that were even possible. Roscoe watched him force himself to take breath after breath before turning back.

'As soon as we get everyone out of here,' he said, speaking directly to Roscoe, 'it's him and us. I will do whatever it takes. I mean that. I don't want him to walk out of here alive.'

Roscoe looked at Savage, remembering his gung-ho approach of the past.

'I hear what you're saying, Peter. We all want to stop the killing. And when we get our man he'll serve his time.'

Savage smiled. 'Always the same, Roscoe. By the book. Surely even you think we should take this one out of the game?'

Before Roscoe had a chance to answer, Anna called across, 'I've got his records here. Richard Winn was employed only at the beginning of last week. He's worked at a couple of London restaurants in the past but nothing special. His reference came directly from Jackson Harlington.'

'Harlington again,' said Roscoe to Savage, knowing for certain each of the three killings was linked. 'Jackson Harlington's the key to this.'

Savage nodded.

'I don't think there's any doubt about that,' he replied. 'Harlington was at the very centre of everything.'

'When the lobby is clear,' said Roscoe, 'we need to prep a unit to head to the fortieth floor.'

'Fortieth floor?' asked Savage.

Roscoe continued, 'I think he's made his way up to the roof. He rode the service elevator from the kitchen all the way to the top of the building. He's planned all of this, Peter. The whole thing.'

'How can you be sure?'

'Because he's been playing with us. He knew who his victims were and picked them off before we had any idea what hit us. And now he wants to take his final bow. But I don't know why. We can't ask Jackson Harlington about Duncan and Winn, so our only hope is to talk to his wife.' He paused. 'Peter, he's waiting for us on the fortieth floor.'

CHAPTER 19

SITTING IN THE STYLISH OFFICE at the rear of the lobby, Jocasta Harlington felt numb. She held her daughter's hand tightly in her own while Oscar Miller, his head bandaged, paced the room, desperately searching for some kind of understanding of what had taken place. In her mind, Jocasta Harlington went over and over what had happened that morning. What had possessed the man to force his way into their suite and why had he targeted Jackson in such a horrific way?

Jocasta had stopped loving her husband many years before. She often told herself she had loved him once, but that was so long ago and for such a short time that it seemed like they were both different people. For years they had lived separate lives and she knew that was an accommodation which suited her just as much as it suited Jackson. She had beautiful homes in Europe and in the United States where she could spend her time with her daughter and with her closest friends. Jackson would spend most of his time at different hotels around the world and they would come together when business demanded. Today was meant to be one of those occasions: she would stand proudly by his side and together they would launch the newest addition to the Tribeca group of luxury hotels.

How could somebody hold such hatred towards Jackson? Jocasta may not have loved her husband but she would never wish such a horrendous fate upon him.

She looked up as Jon Roscoe stepped past the police officer stationed at the entrance to the room and entered the office, along with Anna Conquest.

'Please tell me you've got him, Jon,' she said, greeting Roscoe with a look of desperation.

Roscoe took a seat on the couch next to Jocasta and shook his head.

'There must be some news,' said Oscar Miller, continuing to pace around the room. 'Do you have any idea where he is now? Or who he is?'

Roscoe shook his head again. 'But I think we're making progress,' he said, turning to Jocasta. 'I need your help in trying to understand who we're dealing with.'

In despair, Jocasta held her head in her hands and covered her face.

'Jon, I told you everything when we were upstairs,' she said, lifting her head to look at Roscoe. 'I've no idea who he was.

Honestly, I don't. He said nothing to us the whole time he was in the room.'

'I'm not talking about what happened here today. I need to identify any past links between Mr Harlington and the other men who've been killed.'

'Others?' asked Oscar Miller.

'Two others, I'm afraid, Mr Miller. And in a manner just as brutal.' Roscoe let his words hang in the air. 'The first was a driver, quite possibly the driver who brought you here today.'

'I didn't take much notice of him,' said Miller. 'I arrived on an early flight and he met me at the airport. I was making calls on the drive in and on arrival I went straight up to my suite. I showered and changed and then made my way down to Jackson and Jocasta's a couple of hours later.'

'You didn't take the opportunity to view the hotel?'

'I was here last week. Everything was pretty much done. I spoke to Jackson on the way in and he and I planned to spend some time going over the hotel later this afternoon.'

'And the driver?'

'He arranged for my bags to be taken up to my suite and I didn't see him again. I assume he went into the hotel somewhere.'

Sitting at the oak desk, Anna Conquest listened to the conversation while watching the silent images on the television that hung on the office wall. She never could have imagined the events that had taken place during the day, putting her and Jon at the centre of a global news story. The twenty-four-hour news channels were all running rolling live coverage from outside the hotel. They had obtained some phone footage of Jackson Harlington being held on the balcony of the thirty-eighth floor which was being run over and over. Anna watched the footage and then looked across at Jacqueline Harlington, who was staring at the screen as she saw her father dragged to the front of the balcony. At that point the news network had the decency to cut the clip and Anna watched Jacqueline slowly drop her head. As she did, the news network flashed another 'BREAKING NEWS' banner across the foot of the screen. The image cut away from the exterior of the hotel to a small terraced house in a northern suburb of London. The banner continued, 'New developments in Harlington murder.'

Anna sat forward and clicked up the volume on the television. 'Jon, I think you need to see this.'

Everyone in the room turned their attention to the news reporter standing outside the north London house.

'Right now the timetable of events is pretty unclear,' she began. 'What we do know is a young man and a young woman, both believed to be in their late teens or early twenties, have been freed this morning from a hidden underground basement, where it is believed they have been held captive for the past ten or possibly fifteen years. It is our understanding they were kidnapped when no more than six or seven years old. At this point in time we don't have any identification on them, as police are trying to contact their immediate families, but police sources have told us they are urgently seeking the owner of the house, a Mr Richard Winn. And I can tell you that our own sources have revealed that a possible third captive, who is believed to be two or three years older, was also held with them for the past decade or more. That third captive is believed to have escaped a number of weeks ago and may well have been instrumental in the freeing of the two remaining hostages this morning. And our sources have confirmed to us that that third captive is in his early twenties. He is believed to be Joseph Harlington.'

CHAPTER 20

JOCASTA HARLINGTON DROPPED her head forward, releasing an anguished cry. Her daughter quietly placed her arms around her mother as Oscar Miller stumbled backwards to lean against the office desk. Jon Roscoe looked across at Anna, both of them still trying to comprehend what they had heard. Jon knew he had to speak to Mrs Harlington to try to understand what he was dealing with.

'Mrs Harlington, I need to—'

Jocasta lifted her head, looked first at her daughter and then at Roscoe.

'No, Jon, it's me who needs to talk.' She took a breath, summoning every ounce of her inner strength. 'It was sixteen years ago,' she began, telling a story she had carried with her throughout those years and releasing a pain so deep it had never left her for a single day. 'We were living in London at the time. Tribeca Luxury Hotels was already well established. We had bought all the artificial trimmings which came with that success. The cars, the clothes and an imposing house in Kensington, a short walk from the palace. I soon learnt it was all worth nothing.' She paused, gasping for air.

An intolerable pain shot through Jocasta and she started to sob uncontrollably. She felt her daughter wrap her arms tightly around her before carrying on, falteringly, tears streaking down her face.

'We'd been out late. I'd been drinking but Jackson hadn't, so he'd said he'd drive us. We were at a function for potential investors. Jackson wanted to open a London hotel. We were home so very late. I was exhausted. I went straight upstairs. I never went to bed without checking on Joseph and then Jacqueline. That night I didn't.

'I was asleep in seconds. I remember Jackson getting into bed but nothing more. Next morning I was awake early. I don't know what time it was – probably around five. I was so thirsty. I made my way down to the kitchen and as I did I noticed the outside door was slightly open. I thought it must have been Jackson from the night before but it made me nervous. I went straight back upstairs.' She howled in pain and clasped hold of her daughter's hands. 'Joseph was gone.'

Roscoe nodded. He remembered the case. The Harlingtons were a wealthy family and the press had feasted on the story.

'For months we waited for a ransom demand to tell us Joseph was alive. Something, some kind of contact telling us what they wanted and how we could get Joseph back. But nothing ever came. As time went by, Jackson and the police became convinced he was dead. But I never gave up hope.'

She looked up, and smiled through the tears.

'I knew my son was still alive.'

CHAPTER 21

'I NEED TO ASK you if the two names Michael Duncan and Richard Winn mean anything to you,' asked Roscoe.

'They're the two dead men, aren't they?' Jocasta Harlington said with absolute certainty. 'Michael Duncan was our driver when Joseph was taken. Richard Winn was our chef.' She gave a shallow, bitter laugh. 'We really did have everything money could buy.'

'Did the police question them when Joseph was taken?'

'Everyone was questioned. Over and over. Jackson. Even me.'

'And after the kidnap, what happened to them?' continued Roscoe.

'They stayed around for a while. But I didn't want people coming in and out of the house so Jackson let Winn go pretty quickly. He still needed a driver so I think he kept Duncan on. He never came inside the house again though.'

'I have to ask you this, Mrs Harlington,' Roscoe said, looking at her directly, taking in her ravaged, tear-stained face, 'but did you suspect them?'

She sighed. 'Never directly, but I thought it could have been somebody associated with the business. Or someone who knew us. Everyone knew we had a lot of money but no ransom demand was ever made.'

Roscoe hesitated. 'And Mrs Harlington, I don't like to ask this—'

'Did I ever suspect Jackson was involved?' Jocasta interrupted, and Roscoe knew she was voicing a question she had never dared ask herself for the past sixteen years.

'Did you?'

Jocasta looked at her daughter and then across to Oscar Miller, who still leant against the office desk. Turning back to Roscoe, she said with great certainty, 'No, never.'

'Why not?' he said quickly, aware that he was pushing her but needing answers. 'He employed the driver? He employed the chef?'

'He did.'

'And then Joseph disappeared.'

'Jackson was in bed with me at the time,' Jocasta said sharply, raising her voice. 'Neither of us heard a sound. He would never have done this. Never!'

'But now he's dead. And so is Duncan. And so is Winn.' Roscoe feared he might bully Jocasta into answering but he had to know. 'And from the news report it would seem that Winn had held your son captive for the past sixteen years.'

But Jocasta's head was in her hands again, and Roscoe watched her crying uncontrollably as her daughter held her closely.

The room was silent except for the sounds of Jocasta's sobs and Anna typing on the computer keyboard. Roscoe looked across to her and she gestured for him to come and look at the monitor. She was scanning the original press reports surrounding the case when Joseph had first disappeared.

Four days after their child had been abducted, a press conference was held where the Harlingtons appealed directly to the kidnapper to contact them and let them bring their son home. At the same time, the lead investigating officer made a plea to any member of the public with information surrounding the kidnapping to please come forward.

Anna clicked on the embedded video clip of the press conference.

'If anyone has any information on the kidnapping of Joseph Harlington,' the officer said, 'however small or insignificant they think the information might be, please call the number displayed on the screen now. We have officers waiting to take your calls as I speak. Or, if you prefer, you may ask to speak with me directly.

My name is Detective Sergeant Peter Savage.'

CHAPTER 22

ROSCOE DIVED ACROSS the room and out into the lobby.

'Savage!' he yelled across the vast marbled space, frantically scanning the crowds in front of him. 'Savage, where are you?'

He ran across to the entrance of the hotel, where people were being lined up and counted out as part of the evacuation process. He grabbed hold of the first officer he came across.

'Where's Inspector Savage?' he asked urgently, then repeated, 'Where is Inspector Savage?' with even greater urgency before the officer had a chance to answer.

'He was here a couple of minutes ago,' said the officer, 'but he could see we had everything under control. He said we should continue the evacuation until the foyer was empty.'

Before the officer had finished speaking, Roscoe was sprinting across the lobby. 'Where's the inspector?' he shouted as he ran towards one of the armed officers who'd accompanied him to the twenty-fifth floor.

The officer replied immediately, 'I've been securing the restaurant area, sir. I haven't seen him since we came down in the elevator.'

Bloodied and exhausted but driven on by adrenaline, Roscoe ran back to the reception desk and jumped up onto the counter.

'Savage! Has anyone seen Inspector Savage?'

The crowd assembled in the lobby looked at Roscoe with a mixture of fear and anticipation. In his blood-covered T-shirt, Roscoe realised he looked an alarming sight but he knew he had to find the inspector while he still could. Still standing on top of the reception desk, he turned towards the elevator bank.

The express elevator had stopped at the fortieth floor.

He charged back into the office and knelt down by the couch where Jocasta remained with her daughter.

'Mrs Harlington, I need your help. To stop these killings we must speak to your son.'

'My Joseph?'

Roscoe nodded.

'He was seven years old the last time I saw him. I can't begin to imagine what he's been through.' Jocasta looked desperately at Roscoe, and he wished he could offer her some kind of hope. 'I know what you're thinking, Jon.'

Roscoe put his hand on her arm. 'I'm afraid I'm certain of it. Mrs Harlington, the killer is your son. And the only person who can get him to stop is you.'

CHAPTER 23

TAKING JOCASTA HARLINGTON by the hand, Jon Roscoe led her across the hotel lobby towards the elevator bank. As he did so, he looked across to the entrance of the hotel and saw the evacuees continuing to leave the building. This was almost over.

As they stepped into the express elevator, Jocasta turned to Roscoe.

'I never thought I would see my son again, Jon.'

Roscoe looked across at the mother of a multiple killer. It was impossible for him to imagine how she felt. There were three brutally murdered bodies scattered around the hotel, as well as Stanley fighting for his life in hospital. Her son had been taken from her sixteen years ago and now was about to be returned to her as some kind of avenging executioner.

'I'm terrified, Jon. But at the same time I can't help but feel some kind of anticipation. I'm about to see my son.'

'Even after what he did to Mr Harlington?' Roscoe looked deep into Jocasta's eyes. He felt sure Jackson Harlington had been involved in the boy's kidnap and that was what was driving these revenge attacks.

The elevator doors opened and Roscoe stepped out ahead of Jocasta Harlington. Crossing the glass footbridge that leads from the elevator to the infinity pool, Jocasta stopped.

'Jackson wasn't Joseph's father.'

'Did he know that?' replied Roscoe, startled but not totally surprised as he fit the pieces together in his mind.

'Yes,' she said.

'When did Jackson discover he wasn't Joseph's father?'

'The month before he disappeared.'

Roscoe turned away from Mrs Harlington and looked out across the royal park opposite the hotel. Suddenly it all made sense.

'Jackson was a powerful man, in every sense of the word,' Jocasta said. 'I feared him every second of the day, especially after he found out about Joseph. But although he wasn't Joseph's father, I never believed he would do anything to harm him. I couldn't think that. Ever. Until today.'

A desperate cry came from the other side of the roof terrace and Roscoe quickly ran across the bridge to the shallow end of the pool. What he saw stopped him instantly.

Kneeling at the far end of the pool was the unmasked killer. In front of him, Peter Savage floated in the pool, his throat cut.

Blood traced the water.

The killer gripped Savage by the hair, pulling his head above the water to stop him from drowning and allowing him to slowly bleed to death. Roscoe could see Savage was still alive.

'Joseph. It is Joseph, isn't it?' Roscoe said, the calmness in his voice at odds with the horror rising inside of him. 'This has to stop. Why don't we start by pulling Inspector Savage out of the water?'

He started to take small steps along the edge of the pool, towards Joseph Harlington. As he did, Jocasta came forward and stood motionless by the shallow end. She looked lovingly at her son's face, which bore such a great resemblance to her own, for the first time in sixteen years. Water gently lapped his hands, washing away Savage's blood.

Tension rising within him, Roscoe continued to walk towards the killer. 'Joseph, let's pull Inspector Savage out of the pool.'

When Joseph Harlington looked up and fixed his eyes upon him, Roscoe felt afraid. Never before had he seen such depth of hatred.

'Come one step further and I will blow his brains out.'

As Savage fought for his life, his blood spreading across the pool, Roscoe kept talking. 'Joseph, let's get him out of the water. I can help you.'

Almost imperceptibly he edged forward.

'I told you not to come any further. You should know by now when I say something I mean it.'

And then Joseph ripped a gun from the back of his belt, pressed the barrel into Savage's temple and pulled the trigger.

CHAPTER 24

SAVAGE'S HEAD EXPLODED into the infinity pool. Screaming, Jocasta Harlington collapsed to her knees.

'Joseph, no. No more. Stop this. Please!' she cried.

Standing at the top of the pool, Savage's brains and blood splattered across him, Joseph looked at his mother for the first time.

'I told him not to come any further.' He turned to Roscoe. 'I did tell you not to come any further.'

'Is that it now, Joseph?' asked Roscoe, struck by his child-like logic. 'Have you done what you came to do?'

Still holding the gun, Joseph looked down at Savage's shattered body floating in the pool.

'He was one of them. Every week he would come. Same time each week. He was the worst. He liked to beat me first. And then he'd rape me. He'd make the others watch. And then he'd do the same to them.' He looked at his mother. 'Sixteen years ago he was the one who took me from our house. He loved to tell me that.'

'God help us, Joseph, no more. Let it be over now,' pleaded Jocasta, getting to her feet. 'Please let it be over.'

'He told me how you all moved away. How you'd sold our house. How you didn't live there any more. How I could never go back home. That you didn't want me. Can't you see that for me it can't ever be over?'

'That's not true, Joseph,' Jocasta sobbed. 'I never stopped thinking about you. Every single day. I wanted nothing more than for you to come home. Let me take you home now.' Reaching her arms out to her son, she started to walk slowly down the side of the pool towards him. On the opposite side, Roscoe took his chance to do the same.

'You've got no idea!' Joseph shouted at her. 'We were never let out. Day or night. We were trapped in a dungeon. After Savage, Duncan would only come every couple of months. I always thought he only really got involved for the money. Dad's money.'

Joseph could see his mother stepping forward.

'Don't come any closer!'

He started frantically waving his gun in the direction of first Jocasta and then Roscoe. 'Or you!' he screamed at Roscoe, pointing the weapon directly at him.

'Joseph, this has to stop now,' said Roscoe.

'Winn was there every day, abusing us,' Joseph continued. 'Every single day. Keeping us chained up. Taunting us. Beating us. Telling me every day my father never wanted me.'

'That isn't true!' cried Jocasta.

'But he let them take me. I know he did. They told me. Over and over. He let them take me!'

'No, Joseph,' sobbed Jocasta. 'He wasn't even your father.'

As Joseph turned back to her, Jocasta ran desperately down the side of the pool towards her son.

CHAPTER 25

'STOP!' SHOUTED ROSCOE across the pool, but it was too late.

'He wasn't even your father!' Jocasta was screaming. 'He was an evil, evil man and I'm glad he's dead. He's not part of you and he never was.'

She was standing in front of her son, placing herself at his mercy, as Joseph raised his gun. He pointed it directly at her.

'He wasn't my father?' he asked. 'So that's why he wanted me gone. That's why he let them rape me over and over. That's why he hated me.'

'But he's gone now, Joseph. And I can look after you.'

'It was you who did all this to me. If he had been my father he would have loved me. It's all your fault.'

As Roscoe saw Joseph's finger start to squeeze on the trigger, he hurled himself across the side of the pool, landing on Joseph and knocking him to the ground.

As they fell, the gun fired into the air and flew free.

In a split second Joseph was on his feet and scrambling across the ground to reach the weapon. Roscoe rolled over and up but Joseph already had the gun in his hand. Pointing it at Roscoe and then at his mother, he climbed onto the wall surrounding the infinity pool.

'Joseph, no!' cried Jocasta Harlington, stepping towards her son. 'None of this is your fault. None of it!'

'Stay back. Both of you, stay back or I'll kill you.'

'Let me help you!' screamed Jocasta.

'It's too late, Mum,' he said, stepping to the edge of the wall.

Roscoe charged forward to grab hold of him but, as he did, Joseph opened his arms and fell backwards off the wall of the fortieth floor.

CHAPTER 26

AT THE FRONT of the new Tribeca Luxury Hotel in the Mayfair district of London, a crowd had remained outside throughout the day. The growing numbers of news reporters were joined by members of the public anxious to witness events unfolding. When Joseph Harlington climbed onto the wall surrounding the hotel's infinity pool, cameras and phones were once again pointed skywards. Within minutes, images of him falling through the air and landing on the immaculate lawns of the new hotel were posted online and viewed worldwide. The crowd watched with a mixture of horror and ghoulish delight as Joseph's body hit the ground, close to that of the hotel's owner, Jackson Harlington. Almost immediately, speculation raced around the world that the second body was that of Harlington's missing son, Joseph.

Stepping round the edge of the pool, Roscoe moved towards Jocasta Harlington. Neither of them spoke a word as he put his arms around his employer's widow and she began to sob. As the pair slowly walked away from the poolside, Roscoe turned back and looked one last time at the body of Peter Savage floating in the pool's red water.

Jocasta's daughter, Jacqueline, was standing at the crossing to the glass footbridge.

'It's all over,' Roscoe said to her.

She stepped forward, taking her mother into her arms.

Jocasta Harlington sobbed on to her daughter's shoulder as Roscoe led the pair across the bridge and back to the elevator bank. Standing inside the elevator, he helped Jacqueline support her mother, noticing she had yet to shed a single tear.

When the doors opened to the hotel lobby, almost everyone had been evacuated and the police had taken control. Oscar Miller walked over to help and Roscoe watched as Jacqueline and Miller guided Jocasta across the lobby towards a waiting paramedic.

Anna Conquest was sitting on one of the designer armchairs adorning the lobby. Feeling suddenly exhausted, Roscoe walked over and went to take the seat next to her.

'You'll get blood all over that chair if you sit down in that state. And my guess is that it wasn't cheap.' Anna smiled at Roscoe as he collapsed backwards into the chair. 'You ready for an after-work drink?'

'I'd kill for one,' said Roscoe, 'but there's something I've got to do first.'

CHAPTER 27

ROSCOE WALKED BACK DOWN the two flights of stairs to the hotel control room he had raced up earlier in the day. Fingerprint sensors gave him access to the room and when he entered it seemed almost strange to him that everything was exactly as he had left it. Even his cup of coffee remained untouched. While chaos had reigned across the hotel, the centre of its security operations had remained unscathed.

He logged back into the hotel security systems and began scrolling through the security footage of the past twenty-four hours. He wasn't sure what he was looking for but he knew Joseph Harlington must have had some way of accessing the hotel. And once he was in the hotel, how had he had such extensive knowledge of its layout and who would be where?

Roscoe rubbed his eyes and thought some more. However horrendous Joseph Harlington's past life had been, he had escaped six weeks ago. So where had he been since? And who had helped him? Roscoe felt sure the answers to his questions lay hidden in the security footage.

On screen, Roscoe watched the Harlington family arrive the previous day. Nothing appeared untoward as they were dropped in the hotel parking lot. There was Michael Duncan unloading their bags, leaving them with a bellboy and driving away. Roscoe watched the Harlingtons make their way up through the hotel – across the lobby, a conversation with Anna at reception, walking to the elevators and finally arriving on the twenty-fifth floor. Jackson Harlington led them down the hall to the Royal Garden Suite and all three entered the rooms, the door closing behind them. The suite's private chef accessed its kitchen soon after five, and left a little after nine. And after that, nothing.

Roscoe thought perhaps he was wrong.

He kept scrolling through the footage, but still nothing happened.

Until 3 a.m.

Then the door to the Royal Garden Suite opened.

And out stepped Jacqueline Harlington.

CHAPTER 28

ROSCOE WATCHED JACQUELINE HARLINGTON walk down the hallway, pass the elevator bank and enter the stairwell. After descending twenty-eight flights of stairs, she appeared in the underground parking lot and walked quickly to its staff entrance. Using her father's access-all-areas passcode, she opened the door.

In stepped Joseph.

She hugged him tightly, then brother and sister walked quickly back across the parking lot. Ten minutes later, having climbed the stairs, they appeared on the thirty-eighth floor. Jacqueline followed her brother as he opened the door to the Presidential Suite and the pair disappeared inside. When the time stamp read two minutes after four, Jacqueline exited the room and the door was closed behind her.

Jon Roscoe leant back in his chair. He didn't need to see any more.

CHAPTER 29

Two days later

Stanley Samson was sitting up in his bed in the Chelsea and Westminster Hospital. Beside him in a chair was Aunt Jessie, who had baked him fresh chocolate-frosted doughnuts that morning. Two days before, Stanley had been rushed to the hospital and straight into surgery. He had suffered a substantial loss of blood but luckily his internal organs and stomach had not been severely damaged – seeing Stanley eat his third doughnut, Aunt Jessie was certain of that.

Roscoe put his head round the door. Seeing them both there, he smiled.

'Is everybody decent in here?'

'Jon, come in,' said Aunt Jessie. 'Will you have a doughnut?'

'I'm fine right now, thanks, Aunt Jessie,' he said, sitting on the edge of the bed, 'although it looks like Stanley is more than making up for me.'

They all laughed as Stanley said, 'I've got to build my strength back up.'

'Is that right?' said Roscoe.

'So, what happened?' asked Stanley.

Roscoe had come straight from New Scotland Yard, his old place of work and home to London's Metropolitan Police.

He hesitated for a moment, thinking of the past three days.

'Jon?' asked Aunt Jessie.

'They've questioned Mrs Harlington and Jacqueline. And Oscar Miller. And they wanted me to corroborate everything they've said. It was pretty simple, really. We all saw the same things in the hotel. It would appear that by the time Joseph killed his father, Duncan and Winn were already dead. He'd been waiting for Richard Winn in the kitchen since early in the morning; my guess is he killed him and then hid the body. When you arrived, Aunt Jessie, he was brutalising an already dead man.'

'That man was getting what he deserved,' said Aunt Jessie.

'Probably so,' said Roscoe. 'Michael Duncan had been next on his kill list. After dropping off Oscar Miller, Duncan had gone up to one of the staff bedrooms. Joseph was waiting for him. He had plenty of time to prepare the body and strap it to the chair. Then he had at least two hours to get to Winn's house to free the other hostages. When he got back to the hotel, he waited. Then it was time for the boy who'd been held hostage for the past sixteen years to become the hostage-taker. He waited for Oscar Miller to go down to the Harlingtons' suite and he followed him. And then show time on the balcony. Once he'd killed Jackson Harlington, he headed down the stairs to retrieve Duncan's body and get ready to spin him into the elevator. That's when he ran into you, Stanley.'

'I could have had him, you know, Jon.'

'Less of that,' reprimanded Aunt Jessie. 'He almost killed you, Stanley.'

'And after the kitchen, he made his way up to the fortieth floor. He wanted us to know where he was going as he needed Savage to come after him. He knew Savage would have to – if Joseph walked out of the hotel alive, Savage's life and career were over. The moment Savage saw Michael Duncan spinning in the chair he only had one choice. He had to head up to the pool on his own, as he knew he had to kill Joseph. But Joseph was waiting.'

'What I still don't understand, Jon, is how he was so well prepared,' Aunt Jessie said. 'How did he know his way around the hotel? And where had he been for the last few weeks?'

'Some things we'll never know, Aunt Jessie,' said Roscoe, as he thought of the early-morning security footage he had deleted from record to protect Jacqueline. 'What we do know is Jackson Harlington was a vile man. To be instrumental in what happened to Joseph takes a depth of evil none of us can understand. If he was willing to do that to a boy who was raised as his son, what must he have been doing to his wife and daughter in the years that followed?'

'You're so right,' Aunt Jessie agreed. 'Those poor, poor women.'

'Maybe now their suffering is over and perhaps they can look forward to the future,' said Roscoe. 'The plan is to open the hotel in three weeks' time and there's a lot of work to be done before then. I hope you're going to be fit, Stanley? I'm going to need you to be back at full strength.'

'Don't worry, boss, I'll be back fitter than ever,' said Stanley, taking a bite out of his doughnut.

'I could do with some of your powers of recovery,' laughed Roscoe, turning to Aunt Jessie with a smile. 'You know what? I think I might have one of those doughnuts.'

Can Private's Jack Morgan find a missing royal
before kidnap turns to murder?

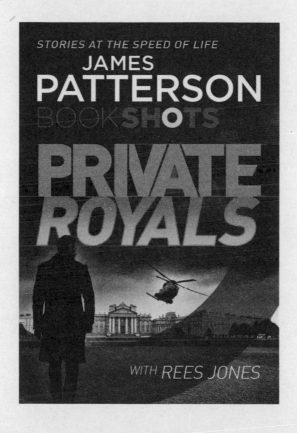

Read on for an extract

AS A FORMER US Marine, an avid traveller, and now head of the world's foremost investigation agency, Jack Morgan had set foot in some of the most grandiose buildings on the planet, and yet he was always taken aback by the majesty of London's iconic architecture.

'Do you know that Horse Guards Parade was first built in 1664?' he asked the man beside him.

'I didn't,' replied Peter Knight, the wiry Englishman who was the head of Private's London office. 'That's over a hundred years older than your country, isn't it?' He smiled and prodded his friend and boss.

'I'd give you a lesson in history now,' Morgan replied, 'but I'm a little outnumbered here.'

Knight laughed as he took in their surroundings. Dozens of British servicemen and women milled beneath the awnings erected at the edge of Horse Guards Parade, but it was champagne flutes that complemented their ceremonial uniforms, not rifles and bayonets.

'Just don't get nervous tomorrow when you see the redcoats.' Knight grinned.

Both he and Morgan wore light summer suits, the June weekend shaping up to be hot and muggy. As a former serviceman himself, Morgan spared a thought for the soldiers who would be standing to attention for hours during the next day's Trooping the Colour parade.

'Glad it's not going to be you on that parade square?' Knight asked, reading his friend's thoughts.

'I'm happier taking in the view, and having this in my hand.' Morgan smiled, holding up his drink. 'I'd be happier still if we were here to secure these events, rather than watching from the sidelines.'

Private had been among a raft of security providers who'd bid for the lucrative contracts to oversee the major events for the Queen's ninetieth birthday celebrations. To Morgan's displeasure, and Knight's embarrassment, Private had not landed a single one.

'It's not on you, Peter,' Morgan told his friend, seeing the slightest of slumps in the Englishman's shoulders. 'This is the old boys' club, and the right school or regiment means more sometimes than service and price.'

Knight nodded his understanding. As a former special investigator to the Old Bailey, he had seen first-hand how Britain's aristocratic class system could still hold sway.

'That's all well and good, Jack, but I don't want people to get hurt because we didn't know a secret handshake.'

'Well, we're here,' Morgan declared brightly, 'so let's enjoy the champagne.'

'Cheers,' Knight offered as the men touched glasses.

'Enjoying the drinks, gentlemen?' they were asked in the nasal tone of the British gentry.

'Colonel De Villiers,' Morgan greeted the Coldstream Guards officer.

At six foot three, Colonel Marcus De Villiers, head of security for the royal family's inner circle, made for an imposing man. He was also the reason why Private had no hand in the security for the Queen's birthday events.

'I'm surprised to see you here, Mr Morgan.' The Colonel's words were neutral, but his eyes betrayed his irritation.

'We were invited,' Knight answered for them.

'Oh.'

Morgan smiled, imagining how the Colonel would be kicking himself inwardly for not having scrutinised the guest list more closely.

A proud man with little time for cocky Americans, De Villiers sneered as he looked at the men's champagne flutes.

'I imagine you made full use of the hospitality provided at the Olympic Games, also? Little wonder that Cronus and his Furies did such damage.' The Colonel was referring to the bloodthirsty murderers who had run amok during the 2012 London Olympics, before finally being brought down by the two men who held their tongues, refusing to take the bait. 'I suppose you did catch him at the closing ceremony, at least.' De Villiers shrugged.

'Peter did, yes, Colonel,' Morgan replied. 'He put his life at risk to save others.' He eyed the thin row of medals on the Colonel's chest and saw none that would signify combat. 'As a military man, I'm sure you would understand all about courage and sacrifice.'

De Villiers was stung by the sarcasm. 'Private investigators should stick to photographing unfaithful spouses, *Mr* Morgan. Good evening.'

The Colonel turned on his heel, and Knight couldn't help but smirk. 'Sounds like someone's made use of that service,' he said.

Morgan laughed and ran a hand through his hair to clear himself of the irritation De Villiers had caused him. As he did so, the American locked eyes with the most beautiful woman present amongst the crowd of cocktail dresses and uniforms.

And she came straight for him.

MORGAN WATCHED AS THE beauty closed the space between them, never once breaking eye contact, confidence radiating from her in waves. Morgan made for a striking figure himself, and was no stranger to women finding him attractive, but even he was a little shocked by the brazen approach that had come from nothing but a look.

'Jane Cook,' the beautiful woman introduced herself, putting out her hand.

Morgan had seen a lot of stunning women in his time, but he didn't know if he'd seen any so attractive when wearing the drab green uniform of the military, and with no make-up.

'Jack Morgan.' He smiled, taking her hand, and quickly ran his eyes over the insignia and decorations of her uniform – she was *Major* Jane Cook of the Royal Horse Artillery, a veteran of Afghanistan and Iraq, and recipient of an OBE.

'I know who you are, Mr Morgan,' she told him. 'I invited you.'

'Jane is a friend of mine,' Knight announced. 'I need to check in with the office. Back in a tick.'

'That's very nice of Peter,' she smiled as Knight took his leave, 'but I'd also like to think of myself as a candidate. I leave the service at the end of the year, Mr Morgan, and I'd like you to be my next employer.'

Realising that the attention towards him was due to business and not pleasure, Morgan almost laughed aloud at his own ego.

'Peter will take care of you, Major, and we'll see if you're the right fit for Private. I'm afraid I'm only here to watch a show. My company has no stake in the celebrations.'

'De Villiers,' Cook said, casting an icy glance towards the man. 'The closest he ever came to combat was an air-conditioned office in Bahrain. I'm sorry you were screwed by him on the contracts, Mr Morgan. I can tell you from personal experience that I know what an institutionalised old boys' club the British security forces can be.'

'Call me Jack. And it is what it is. Believe me, there are cliques and fraternities in the American hierarchy too.'

'So what brings you here to London, if not work?' she asked.

'Heading back from Europe across the pond, so I wanted to see how my guys are getting along here. I've always wanted to see the Trooping the Colour parade, so when Peter told me that he had invitations, I could hardly refuse.'

'Well, I'm glad you'll get to experience something new here in London.' Cook's eyes gave the slightest suggestion that marching soldiers were not all the city had to offer. 'Home is LA?'

'The Palisades. It's the bit between LA and Malibu.'

'Malibu? Do you surf?'

'It's the second-best way I know to clear my head.' Morgan smiled.

Cook fought a losing battle to stop herself from doing the same. 'I surf. In Cornwall,' she managed, on the edge of blushing.

Morgan said nothing. His own smile was gone.

Because Knight was on his way back in a hurry, and Morgan recognised the look on his friend's face.

'They need us at headquarters,' Knight informed his boss. 'Now.'

WITH MORGAN ON HIS shoulder, Knight pushed open the door to his office in Private London's headquarters.

Neither of them were surprised to see the grey-haired gentleman inside.

He stood at the window, looking out over the city, his hands clasped behind a bespoke tailored suit. His outward appearance suggested calm and confidence, even when standing alone inside a stranger's office. It was an appearance that would fool almost anybody.

But Jack Morgan and Peter Knight were not just anybody, and they could see the tension in the man's posture and hear his exaggerated breathing.

They knew who he was, of course – no one could waltz into Private, let alone Knight's office, without the say-so of someone in a position of authority. Knight had granted his because his workspace was sterile, all files deeply encoded on drives that were unobtainable unless the man at the window had been a master hacker.

And he was not. He was the ageing Duke of Aldershot, and a member of the royal family.

'Sir,' Knight said simply, and the man turned towards them.

On the journey from Horse Guards, a quick Internet search had revealed the Duke to be sixty years old. However, with his red eyes and pale skin, the royal looked closer to a hundred.

'Please, sir, take a seat,' Knight offered, worried that the man was moments from collapse. Without a word, the Duke complied.

Morgan hung back by the door as Knight poured the Duke a glass of water and pulled his own chair forward so that he was at arm's length from him.

'I can get tea or coffee if you like, sir?' Knight asked. The Duke shook his head and the water remained untouched, trembling in his hands.

'Your Grace,' Knight began, patiently, 'we know who you are, and whatever the problem is, we can help you with it. Why are you here?'

The Duke's haunted eyes showed the first signs of life.

'Abbie,' he mumbled.

'Your daughter?' Knight asked, recognising her name from his Internet search on the Duke. 'Is she in trouble?'

The Duke nodded slowly, a pair of tears racing down his pale cheeks. 'Yes,' he gasped.

'How do you know, sir?' Morgan asked from the doorway.

The Duke's eyes widened as he turned towards the American's voice.

'I will show you.'

CHANGED INTO HIS STREET clothing of jeans and a roll-sleeved shirt, Knight pulled the Range Rover to a stop at Chelsea Harbour, the Duke and a hoody-wearing Morgan emerging from its back seat. The ride had been quiet, the investigators wanting to hold their questions for the Duke until they had set eyes on what he assured them was the scene of a crime.

'Nice place,' Morgan said quietly to Knight, casting his eyes across the rows of moored boats. 'He says hers is the centre penthouse.' He pointed at a block of luxury apartments.

'Wonder what the rent is on that,' Knight said.

'About seven million to buy.'

Knight was about to ask Morgan how he knew, but the confident smile of the handsome man told him the full story.

'Leave some for the rest of us, will you?' Knight grinned, turning to see a white transit van pull up behind the Range Rover.

'The cavalry has arrived,' the van's driver announced from its window in an east London accent.

'Good to see you, Hooligan.' Morgan smiled, extending his hand to the man who was the guru when it came to all things forensic, scientific and technological at Private London.

'Good to see you too, Jack.'

'Your Grace, this is Jeremy Crawford,' Knight introduced the scruffy man more formally.

'Call me Hooligan, Duke' he insisted. Red-haired and freckled, the self-confessed geek had earned the nickname for his love of all things West Ham, and wore the moniker as a badge of honour.

The Duke said nothing, and seemed to shrink at the sight of the building in front of them.

'It's OK, sir. The sooner you take us inside, the sooner we can make sure your daughter's safe.'

Morgan wanted to reassure the Duke. But once they'd entered the building and gone into the penthouse apartment, he feared he may have spoken too soon.

The room was awash with blood.

'Bloody 'ell,' Hooligan exclaimed before catching himself. 'I'll get to work on some samples then, shall I?'

'Do it,' Morgan agreed, then turned to Knight. 'Peter. Elaine still at Scotland Yard?' Elaine was the sister of Knight's deceased wife, and was a well-respected inspector on London's Metropolitan Police Force.

'Want me to call it in?'

'No police!' the Duke said urgently, coming alive. 'He'll kill her!' He pointed a shaking finger at the kitchen countertop.

Morgan stepped carefully to it, and cast his eyes over the granite.

A message had been scrawled in blood:

'I HAVE YOUR DAUGHTER.'

JAMES PATTERSON
BOOK SHOTS
OUT THIS MONTH

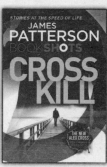

Along Came a Spider killer Gary Soneji died years ago. But Alex Cross swears he sees Soneji gun down his partner. Is his greatest enemy back from the grave?

Humans are evolving into a savage new species that could save civilisation – or end it. *Zoo* was just the beginning.

Detective Harry Blue is determined to take down the serial killer who's abducted several women, but her mission leads to a shocking revelation.

A royal is kidnapped the day before the Trooping the Colour parade. Can Private's Jack Morgan save the day before kidnap turns to murder?

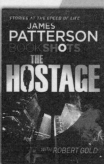

A world-famous tennis player is stalked from Roland Garros to Wimbledon by a deadly killer intent on destroying more than just her career.

Two rival crews attempt to steal millions of pounds' worth of diamonds at exactly the same time, leading to a thrilling high-speed chase across Europe.

When former SAS captain David Shelley goes looking for a missing friend, he enters into the same danger that may have got his friend killed.

A man is thrown from the top floor of a glamorous new London hotel. Can Head of Security John Roscoe find the killer before the bodies pile up?

JAMES
PATTERSON
BOOK SHOTS
COMING SOON

AIRPORT: CODE RED

A major terrorist cell sets a devastating plan in motion.
Their target? One of the world's busiest airports.

THE TRIAL: A WOMEN'S MURDER CLUB THRILLER

An accused killer will do anything to disrupt his own trial, including
a courtroom shocker that Lindsay Boxer will never see coming.

LITTLE BLACK DRESS

Can a little black dress change everything? What begins
as one woman's fantasy is about to go too far.

LEARNING TO RIDE

City girl Madeline Harper never wanted to love a cowboy. But rodeo
king Tanner Callen might change her mind... and win her heart.

ALSO BY JAMES PATTERSON

ALEX CROSS NOVELS

Along Came a Spider
Kiss the Girls
Jack and Jill
Cat and Mouse
Pop Goes the Weasel
Roses are Red
Violets are Blue
Four Blind Mice
The Big Bad Wolf
London Bridges
Mary, Mary
Cross
Double Cross
Cross Country
Alex Cross's Trial (*with Richard DiLallo*)
I, Alex Cross
Cross Fire
Kill Alex Cross
Merry Christmas, Alex Cross
Alex Cross, Run
Cross My Heart
Hope to Die
Cross Justice

THE WOMEN'S MURDER CLUB SERIES

1st to Die
2nd Chance (*with Andrew Gross*)
3rd Degree (*with Andrew Gross*)

4th of July (*with Maxine Paetro*)
The 5th Horseman (*with Maxine Paetro*)
The 6th Target (*with Maxine Paetro*)
7th Heaven (*with Maxine Paetro*)
8th Confession (*with Maxine Paetro*)
9th Judgement (*with Maxine Paetro*)
10th Anniversary (*with Maxine Paetro*)
11th Hour (*with Maxine Paetro*)
12th of Never (*with Maxine Paetro*)
Unlucky 13 (*with Maxine Paetro*)
14th Deadly Sin (*with Maxine Paetro*)
15th Affair (*with Maxine Paetro*)

DETECTIVE MICHAEL BENNETT SERIES

Step on a Crack (*with Michael Ledwidge*)
Run for Your Life (*with Michael Ledwidge*)
Worst Case (*with Michael Ledwidge*)
Tick Tock (*with Michael Ledwidge*)
I, Michael Bennett (*with Michael Ledwidge*)
Gone (*with Michael Ledwidge*)
Burn (*with Michael Ledwidge*)
Alert (*with Michael Ledwidge*)

PRIVATE NOVELS

Private (*with Maxine Paetro*)
Private London (*with Mark Pearson*)

Private Games (*with Mark Sullivan*)

Private: No. 1 Suspect (*with Maxine Paetro*)

Private Berlin (*with Mark Sullivan*)

Private Down Under (*with Michael White*)

Private L.A. (*with Mark Sullivan*)

Private India (*with Ashwin Sanghi*)

Private Vegas (*with Maxine Paetro*)

Private Sydney (*with Kathryn Fox*)

Private Paris (*with Mark Sullivan*)

NYPD RED SERIES

NYPD Red (*with Marshall Karp*)

NYPD Red 2 (*with Marshall Karp*)

NYPD Red 3 (*with Marshall Karp*)

NYPD Red 4 (*with Marshall Karp*)

STAND-ALONE THRILLERS

Sail (*with Howard Roughan*)

Swimsuit (*with Maxine Paetro*)

Don't Blink (*with Howard Roughan*)

Postcard Killers (*with Liza Marklund*)

Toys (*with Neil McMahon*)

Now You See Her (*with Michael Ledwidge*)

Kill Me If You Can (*with Marshall Karp*)

Guilty Wives (*with David Ellis*)

Zoo (*with Michael Ledwidge*)

Second Honeymoon (*with Howard Roughan*)

Mistress (*with David Ellis*)

Invisible (*with David Ellis*)

The Thomas Berryman Number

Truth or Die (*with Howard Roughan*)

Murder House (*with David Ellis*)

NON-FICTION

Torn Apart (*with Hal and Cory Friedman*)

The Murder of King Tut (*with Martin Dugard*)

ROMANCE

Sundays at Tiffany's (*with Gabrielle Charbonnet*)

The Christmas Wedding (*with Richard DiLallo*)

First Love (*with Emily Raymond*)

OTHER TITLES

Miracle at Augusta (*with Peter de Jonge*)